"Still wild enough to swim naked with me?" Yannis asked Cara

"What do you think?" She crossed her forearms under her breasts, offering them up to him.

As he stared, her nipples tightened further, and he didn't think it was from the cool night breeze. "I think yes." As if of its own accord, his hand rose and hovered above her right breast.

She pulled his hand to her. They gasped simultaneously. Her breast filled his palm, full and heavy like an apple ripe for the picking. He instinctively thumbed her nipple, making her shudder.

Encouraged, he cupped her other breast, teasing and plucking. She tipped back her head. "Oh, Yannis."

He'd never felt skin so soft, so smooth before and closed his eyes in sheer sensual pleasure. Then suddenly his hands were empty.

Cara had stepped back from him and dropped the rest of her dress to the sand. She spun on her heel and ran toward the ocean, wearing only a tiny pair of black panties. "Last one in is a rotten egg!" she cheerfully called over her shoulder.

She'd literally pulled heaven from his grasp and now she called him a rotten egg? Yannis stripped down _____ _____ _____ after her. Never mind _____ _____ ___ her screaming his in___

Dear Reader,

In a funny way, I've been waiting to write a book about Greece since I was a kid. My grandparents on my dad's side were both organic chemists. My grandmother was one of the first women to earn her PhD in organic chemistry from Columbia University and ran a defense lab during World War II, where she was burned in an explosion. She decided to stay home after the war to raise her kids, writing chemistry books and articles with my grandfather. The only words in these articles I ever understood were *a, and* and *the*.

Once they retired, my grandfather decided to learn Greek. Not the useful, modern Greek language, as in "I'd like to order gyros," but ancient Greek, so he could read Homer's *Odyssey*. In the original. So he did. Over the years he and my grandmother took several trips to Greece and brought me a marble statue of Athena, goddess of wisdom, which I still have. One of my favorite memories is snuggling in bed with my grandma as she quizzed me in Greek mythology.

So here is my tribute to my grandparents and the Greece they loved. I hope you enjoy Cara's story as she falls in love with Yannis and learns to love his homeland, as well.

Marie Donovan

P.S. I'm delighted to hear from my readers. Visit www.mariedonovan.com to learn more about my upcoming books.

My Sexy
Greek Summer

MARIE DONOVAN

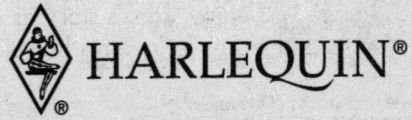

HARLEQUIN®

TORONTO • NEW YORK • LONDON
AMSTERDAM • PARIS • SYDNEY • HAMBURG
STOCKHOLM • ATHENS • TOKYO • MILAN • MADRID
PRAGUE • WARSAW • BUDAPEST • AUCKLAND

Recycling programs
for this product may
not exist in your area.

ISBN-13: 978-0-373-79474-4
ISBN-10:   0-373-79474-6

MY SEXY GREEK SUMMER

Copyright © 2009 by Marie Donovan.

www.eHarlequin.com

Printed in U.S.A.

ABOUT THE AUTHOR

Marie Donovan is a Chicago-area native, who got her fill of tragedies and unhappy endings by majoring in opera/vocal performance and Spanish literature. As an antidote to all that gloom, she read romance novels voraciously throughout college and graduate school.

Donovan graduated magna cum laude with two bachelor's degrees from a Midwestern liberal arts university and speaks six languages. She worked for a large suburban public library for ten years as both a cataloguer and a bilingual Spanish story-time presenter. She enjoys reading, gardening and yoga.

Books by Marie Donovan

HARLEQUIN BLAZE
204—HER BODY OF WORK
302—HER BOOK OF PLEASURE
371—BARE NECESSITIES

To my grandmother and my grandfather.

1

"LOOK AT HOW BEAUTIFUL this place is, Cara! I can't believe you didn't want to come."

Cara Sokol elbowed her friend in the ribs from where they were leaning on the ferry railing. Emma Taylor's cheerful voice had carried to the clumps of locals. The ones who understood English looked at Cara with marked unfriendliness.

Welcome to Greece. As if Cara needed another reason for the Greek populace to hate her. "Aphrodisias is as beautiful as its namesake," she told Emma loudly.

At her compliment to their admittedly lovely island, the scowlers turned to gaze at the landmass they were approaching. Cara poked her friend in the ribs again. "Emma, enough about my not wanting to come to Greece. I never said it wasn't a beautiful country."

"Sorry, Cara." Emma swiped a hunk of straight blond hair out of her face.

Cara had expected the wild sea winds on the ferry ride and had pulled her curly red hair back into a braid. She couldn't get a comb through her hair on a good day, and the June Aegean trade winds would snarl her hair into a copper-wire scouring pad. "That's okay. I know you're excited about our trip."

"Well, who wouldn't be?" Emma gestured broadly at

the vista in front of them. "Greece—the cradle of mathematics, the birthplace of Euclid, Pythagoras, Archimedes—did you know that before Archimedes died at the siege of Syracuse, he requested his favorite mathematical proof be carved on his tomb?"

"Wow." Cara would be hard-pressed to think of an appropriate proof for her own tomb. Maybe a big, fat zero with a slash through it, but she didn't even know the fancy math name for it. She shook off her Greek-induced grumpiness and instead stared ahead. Emma was still talking about Greek mathematicians, understandably since she was a Ph.D. student in math at the University of Michigan in Ann Arbor, where they were neighbors in the same apartment building. Emma looked like a cuddly blond cheerleader but had the brain of a supercharged computer.

While Emma subsided into silence with a happy sigh, Cara fell into the rhythm of the Greek speakers, their rapid-fire consonants and vowels sorting out into words as her ears adjusted to the language. The older men were complaining about ever-volatile Greek politics and the crooks mismanaging things in Athens, the women were discussing children and clothes, and the two young men closest to Cara and Emma were commenting on the girls passing by.

Cara hid a smile as the guys wondered if she and Emma dyed their hair and discussed their hip size in favorable terms. Chauvinistic Greek men might be, but at least they liked girls with some meat on their bones.

She straightened from the railing and let her gaze travel casually over the two young men. She knew better than to wink at them, since she didn't want them following her around Aphrodisias like eager puppy dogs. They met her gaze and grinned, obviously enjoying the idea of putting one over on the foreign girl. *Sorry, dudes, I've been there and done that.* She'd like to meet the Greek guy who could put one over on her now.

Despite her previous travels in Greece, Cara had never been to Aphrodisias, part of the Cyclades group of islands. The island was straight out of Greek legend, craggy hills where undoubtedly shepherds still tended their flocks, blindingly white cubic houses dotting the town and a wide crescent of sandy beach pouring out into the ocean.

Emma followed her gaze. "Oh my gosh, look at that beach! As soon as we get settled, I am going to practically live there."

"Athena says that beach is where the goddess Aphrodite first came ashore. That's why the island is named after her."

"Amazing." Emma's eyes gleamed with anticipation. "A whole island named after the Greek goddess of love? I can hardly wait to find out what kind of men must live here."

Cara could. She had things to do other than cruise around Aphrodisias for Greek men. Visit Athena, for one. She sighed quietly but Emma heard her anyway.

"Oh, hey, here I am blabbing about guys like we're on spring break in Florida and you must be worrying about your friend. What did her daughter-in-law tell you when you called from Athens?"

Cara shrugged. "Oh, Demetria says Athena is still having complications since they brought her home from the hospital. It wasn't so much the broken hip, but the pulmonary embolism she got after the surgery. They're having trouble making sure she doesn't get another clot. Athena refuses to go back to the hospital, so they're limited in what they can do for her."

Emma patted her back. "Nasty stuff. But I'm sure she'll

recover quickly now that she's home." Emma stared out at the island. "There's something about this place…but I don't know what."

Cara stared at Aphrodisias. The island was something, all right. Home to the only person in the world who could get her to return to Greece.

"IS SHE HERE? Is she here?" Athena Kefalas pulled herself to her feet using the aluminum-frame walker her doctor insisted on. Walkers were for old ladies, bah! And Athena Kefalas was not an old lady at seventy. Hadn't her own dear mother lived to ninety-five and just passed away last year, God rest her soul, *O Theos na tin anapafsi.* She shook out her long black skirt and clumped over to the kitchen, where Demetria was hanging up the phone.

Her daughter-in-law pursed her lips and blinked a couple times, no doubt to get some patience with her mother-in-law. As far as Athena was concerned, she was a model mother-in-law compared to her own Giorgy's mother. Now *she* had been a mother-in-law straight from the Evil One himself. *She* had also lived to a ripe old age, probably because the *daimones* were afraid to have her in Hell. They had eventually relented, though, and no doubt welcomed her as one of their own.

Ah, but perhaps Athena *was* getting old, reminiscing about long ago and not focusing on the present. And more importantly, the future. "Demetria, did Karoleena arrive?"

"Yes, Mother, she and her friend arrived at the villa you arranged for them and will come to see you this afternoon. But remember, Karoleena wants us to call her Cara, her American name."

"Of course, of course." Athena nibbled at a dish of

pickled olives on the sturdy kitchen table. "And when *Cara* and her friend come, they must think I am still sick."

Demetria snorted. "You may need that walker for a couple more weeks, but you look as healthy as a lamb in springtime."

"Hmm." Athena frowned. "I need to be pale and sickly. Demetria, bring me the flour."

"Flour? Why? Are we baking *kourabiethes* for Cara?"

Athena paused for a second. Karoleena did love the sugared almond cookies, but no time for baking now. "To powder my face, of course. If Karoleena knows I am well, she will leave quickly and she *needs* to be here on Aphrodisias."

Demetria didn't bother to ask why again but brought the flour.

Athena looked up from where she was patting the white powder into her overly healthy-looking cheeks. "Thank you, Demetria. You are a good daughter."

"Now, Mother, you only say that when you want me to do something."

"Actually, if you could loan me your gray eye makeup to put circles under my eyes…"

Demetria blew out a breath strong enough to rival the ocean breeze but left to fetch the eye shadow.

Athena stared out the kitchen window overlooking the beach from where the Goddess of Love had appeared. So little love in this world anymore. But Athena had always known best, especially since her own dear mother had named her after the Goddess of Wisdom. She would do anything to help Karoleena, her poor girl who was so unhappy. And if Athena needed to wear enough flour on her face to make *kourabiethes* for the whole island, then by Aphrodite, she would!

CARA FINISHED UNPACKING her clothes into the dresser and took a deep breath. Athena, or probably Demetria, had chosen well in their vacation villa. The apartment was large and airy with whitewashed walls and pale gray marble floor tiles throughout. The furniture was solid dark walnut and would take a team of strapping Greek youths to move.

She walked into the big living room with a long, burnt-orange, L-shaped sectional couch and stared at the large weaving hanging on the wall. She'd seen Athena's work often enough to know it was either hers or someone whom she'd taught. It had the look of an ancient Greek textile with its black figures on a red background, but the subject matter was typical of Athena—Artemis, the goddess of the hunt chasing down some man who had offended her. There was even a tiny arrow sticking out of the offender's butt.

Cara giggled, her first laugh since landing in Athens. Emma, coming out of her own room, saw her smiling at the weaving. "Now that's more like it. Isn't this place great? That breeze blowing through the windows—and look, a balcony." Emma hurried to the French doors and threw them open. "The flowers are amazing, and the sea beyond."

Cara followed her onto the balcony. It held a small tiled table and two chairs overlooking bright blue–painted window boxes. Masses of bougainvillea trailed from the boxes down the side of the building, their ruffled fuchsia flowers soft and delicate against the spiky dark green leaves. Prim pink geraniums stood upright as if to reprimand their lazy sisters for falling over. She inhaled a deep breath of their sweet fragrance mixed with the salty air. The startlingly blue Aegean glittered in front of them.

"I'm getting my camera." Emma rushed back to her

room and returned with her small digital camera. "Say cheese, Cara."

Something loosened in her stomach. This was what she loved about Greece—the open sea; the flowers; the crisp, pure air, where the sun shone differently than it did anywhere else. Cara grinned at the camera and Emma took her picture.

"Now take mine." They switched places and then Emma took several more photos of the harbor view.

Cara wandered back into the villa's kitchen to pull two mineral waters from the small fridge. "Here, be sure to drink something. We haven't had much chance since we got into Athens, and the long plane ride dries you out."

"Thanks. Cheers." Emma clinked her bottle against Cara's. "Or should I say *'Opa!'* and fling my bottle against the wall?"

"I don't think the maid would like that. But if you want, we can find a tourist restaurant where they fling plates and dance around like Anthony Quinn in *Zorba the Greek.*"

"And of course that's a terrible stereotype since Greeks don't like to dance?" Emma lifted a blond eyebrow.

Cara grinned. "Of course they do." She drank her *metaleekó neró* and stared at the ocean. She loved the sea— ironic, since she now lived in Michigan, a thousand miles from the nearest salt water. She spotted a sail on the horizon and her heart quickened. "Look, Emma, a sailboat."

"That's right, you used to crew on sailboats before you moved to Michigan. Getting paid to sail the ocean blue must have been a great gig."

"I did travel all over—California, Mexico, the Caribbean, even once around Corfu—that's one of the western Greek islands more influenced by Italy." She changed the subject hurriedly. "Anyway, we should go sailing if we have time. Maybe Athena has a cousin who can take us out on the water."

"Great! Speaking of Athena, isn't she expecting us now?" Emma checked her leather-banded watch.

Cara laughed. "You may as well take that thing off. Greek time doesn't work the same as American time. Athena is expecting us sometime this afternoon. And if we don't show up until evening, she'll just feed us then."

Emma set down her empty bottle. "Greek time or no, I want to go explore the town. Ready?"

Cara nodded and followed, grabbing her wide-brimmed hat and sunglasses. She locked the villa and they descended the narrow stone stairs down to street level. "Athena's house is only supposed to be a half mile away. If we get lost, everyone knows where she lives."

It was a slow half mile, with Emma stopping frequently to admire the cobalt-blue front doors and shutters and masses of pink and purple flowers. When they emerged into the sun from the shadowed back streets, Cara popped her hat and sunglasses on.

Emma glanced over at her. "You're not going to get any color at all if you keep bundling up." She tipped her face up to the blazing afternoon sun and chuckled happily.

"And *you* are going to spend your vacation crying on the couch from sun poisoning. This isn't Michigan, you know. The sun is much stronger and you get a triple dose when it bounces off the water and sand."

"I don't suppose there's any way we can pass for locals anyway, is there?" Emma sent her a teasing glance.

"Not many redheaded Greek women out there." Cara smiled at her friend. She could have been the county fair Corn Queen for her Midwestern looks, a far cry from the supertanned blond beach bunny often spotted at topless beaches around the country.

Emma said theatrically, "Alas, alas, I'll just have to be the legendary American co-ed on summer vacation." She looked around in delight. They were now in the center of town and passing quaint tavernas and sidewalk cafés. "But I thought there'd be more people around. You did say summers were crowded in the Cyclades."

Cara studied the scene, spotting cameras and white limbs sticking out from shorts and tank tops. "The locals are probably home napping. They often have a siesta time, especially in the summer. Everybody else is a tourist."

"Including us." Emma laughed. "But we have to hit the club tonight. On a Friday night it should be pretty lively, right?"

"Definitely." Seemed as if they were in for a girls' night out. Emma wasn't used to Greek guys and didn't speak more than five words of the language. Cara snickered to herself. Too bad Cara didn't have the long black clothes and black beady glare typical of an old widowed aunt protecting her naive charge from the big, bad men of the world.

"Doesn't that sound fun, Cara?"

Actually, it did. Cara had loved going out on the town, particularly to a raucous Greek nightspot. "Sure, but don't forget we're still getting over jet lag."

"Yes, Mother. Wait, how do you say that in Greek?"

"Ne, meetéra."

Emma repeated it with an accent awful enough to make Cara groan. "Let's practice your Greek after lunch."

Emma waved her hand. "No thanks, I'll practice on one of those Greek men tonight."

"And they'll be happy to let you." Cara turned a corner and checked her directions. "Here we are." Suddenly sick with anxiety, she pressed her hand against her stomach.

She'd never been good around illness, and Athena was one of her best friends.

"Easy, Cara." Emma must have picked up on her panic. "Take a couple deep breaths and we'll see how she is." Emma reached around her and knocked on the door. "I wonder why all the doors and window shutters are painted blue."

"To keep out the Evil Eye," Cara replied automatically, clicking back into tour guide mode. "It all dates to ancient times...." She continued talking until Demetria threw open the door and beckoned them into the narrow stone-tiled foyer.

"Karoleena, is that really you?" She pulled Cara to her bosom, kissing her heartily on each cheek. "Your hair, it's so red and—how you say?—fluffy?"

"Emma, this is Demetria, Athena's daughter-in-law," Cara called to her friend as Demetria fussed over her.

"Oh, look at you! So round and healthy!" Demetria eyed Cara's breasts and hips, which had expanded a bit since they last met. "You're eating now!"

Time to change the subject. "Demetria, this is my friend Emma Taylor. She was kind enough to come to Aphrodisias with me."

"Emma!" Demetria fell on a startled Emma with the same fervor with which she'd greeted Cara. After kissing Emma on the cheeks, she pulled back. "Another lovely girl! And so fair!" She pinched Emma's cheek. "The boys here will love you. If only my son Spiro wasn't away for the summer. A pretty blond American—he'll be heartbroken he missed you."

"Demetria..." an old voice quavered from a room beyond.

"Is that Athena?" Cara tried to control her nervousness, meanwhile, Demetria's cheerful expression had turned grim.

"Yes. We're coming," she called. "Mother has been anxious to see you." She ushered them into a sitting room where Athena lay on a couch, swathed in blankets.

Cara bit back a gasp. Her old friend looked terrible, pale and shadowed. "Oh, Athena, how are you?" She reached for Athena's hand, and Athena grasped hers with surprising strength.

"Better, now that you are here."

Cara looked over her shoulder at Demetria for confirmation. Demetria nodded. "It's a miracle how much better she is."

Athena let out a little moan and Cara spun back to her. "I'm glad to see you again," she said soothingly. "And Aphrodisias is even more beautiful than you described."

Athena nodded. "My birthplace, the place I knew I would return to in my old age. The place to fulfill my dream of a museum of Greek island weaving and other women's arts."

"When you feel better, you can work on your project."

Athena's black eyes went wide. "I was just about to purchase the perfect property when I fell and broke my hip. I was at the market and stepped on an olive. An olive, I tell you! I have been walking on my own two feet for over sixty-five years and a miserable olive trips me." She lapsed into Greek and muttered several imprecations against that hapless squished fruit.

Emma looked blankly at Cara and Cara shrugged. Those weren't words Emma needed to practice for polite conversation. "Emma, come meet my friend Athena."

Cara made the introductions and Emma shook Athena's hand gently. "Thank you for inviting me to come with Cara. I have nothing but the highest respect for the Greek land and its wonderful history of mathematics."

Athena nodded regally, accepting all honors to Euclid, Pythagorus & Co. as her due. "Would you like to see Demetria's lovely garden? The flowers are beautiful, thanks to a wet spring."

Emma agreed and followed Demetria toward the end of the house, leaving Cara and Athena together.

Athena continued in Greek. "Karoleena, your friend speaks Greek?"

"Oxi." Cara shook her head.

"Good. How does she think you and I know each other?"

"I told her I was working on a cruise ship through the islands and let her assume we met that way."

"And that is all she knows?" Gone was the sick old lady, and in her place was the woman spearheading a new museum.

"Yes, Athena." Cara checked Emma's whereabouts, her voice faded as she went into the courtyard garden.

"Fine. I will keep your privacy, if that is what you wish."

"Efkhareestó, Athena."

"You're welcome, *chriso mou.*" Athena smiled up at her with such sweetness that Cara bent down and hugged her gently. *Chriso mou*—my golden one. It had been so long since she'd heard those words. Athena patted her on the back.

"I'm glad you're feeling better."

Athena heaved a sigh. "Yet not well enough to continue my project, which is why I need you."

Cara sat up on the edge of the couch. "Me? What do I know about building a museum?"

Her friend waved a negligent hand. "You will be my eyes and ears. Just some minor details to finish, and if the men do not know you understand Greek, so much the better."

"Athena…" Cara stood. "I only came to Aphrodisias because you were so sick and I wanted to make sure you were getting better. I wasn't planning to stay."

"Do you have a job in America you need to return to?" Athena raised an eyebrow.

Cara paced across the room. Stay in Greece? "No, but I'm taking classes at the university."

"During the summer?"

"Well, kind of." Athena gave her one of those baleful black stares older Greek women had perfected. "Well, they start in September, which is technically summer, at least until the twenty-first." Cara never could lie to Athena.

"September? *Pfft*. It's only June. And your friend Emma can stay, as well, unless she has a job."

"No, she can work on her studies from here." Cara looked out the window facing the courtyard. Emma was having a ball, sniffing the flowers and laughing at whatever Demetria was telling her. "Summer in Greece?" she murmured.

"It will do you good. Put some color in your cheeks and take that frown off your face."

Cara made an effort to smile. Poor her. A summer on an idyllic Greek island with nothing to do but help an old, ailing friend. Boo hoo.

"Ah, that's better." Athena struggled to her elbows and smiled up at her. "Now come here for a kiss and have Demetria make us some coffee."

Cara kissed Athena on both cheeks as she was bid and then sneezed. Something dusty was tickling her nose.

"*Yia sou*," Athena blessed her.

"Thanks." Cara sniffled and sought out Emma and Demetria in the garden.

Emma predictably squealed in glee at the idea of a Greek summer but then got a worried look on her face. "Be sure to tell me how much I owe you for rent and groceries, that kind of thing."

Cara exchanged glances with Demetria. "Don't worry about the money. We'll get a deal since it's a long-term rental."

"Great!" Emma hugged her and pulled away. "Cara, you have some white stuff in your hair." Emma brushed it out.

"Probably some dust or sand. So you girls are staying for the summer!" Demetria hugged them and pinched their cheeks again.

"Anything to help Athena."

Demetria led them into the kitchen and began measuring cold water into the small metal coffeepot. "With you here, I think my mother-in-law will recover faster than you expect."

2
___

"IS THAT TRUE, CARA, what Athena said about Aphrodisias?"

Cara blinked as Emma's voice penetrated the late-afternoon haze as they stretched out on beach towels on the warm, sun-drenched sand. "Hmmm?" She took off her floppy sun hat and raised her head from where she'd been cradling it on her forearms.

Emma had been lying on her back in a tiny lavender-purple bikini but she'd propped herself up on her elbows. "You know, about the island being a magnet for lovers?"

Cara gestured to the surrounding beach. "It's a popular vacation spot. People either bring their lovers or find a new one here." She and Emma were practically the only non-romantic couple there. Pretty girls were snuggling with men, from potential male underwear models to men who should have had their banana-hammock swimsuits confiscated by Greek border security before they even entered the country.

Cara winced at one particularly gray and hairy dude in a neon-orange bikini bottom, the color of a traffic hazard cone. *Warning, warning, hazardous materials, stay away...*

Emma continued, "Athena said there was more to it than just fun and sun. She said the old ways still hold sway here."

"I suppose that's fair to say of many of the islands. Like

you asked me before, the blue paint on doors and roofs is to block the Evil Eye, and some of the old gods were folded into Christian customs. That's probably what Athena meant."

"Maybe. But while you were in the kitchen with Demetria making coffee, she said that those who have been unlucky in love would always find love on Aphrodisias."

"What?" Cara rolled onto her side and sat up. "What does that mean?"

Emma shrugged. "Something about Aphrodite taking pity on losers in the game of love."

Great. Not only was Cara a loser pitied by her friend Athena, but also pitied by an ancient Greek goddess. "Are you looking to get lucky in love here?" Cara sure wasn't.

"Love?" Emma pursed her lips thoughtfully. "I think I'd settle for sex at this point."

Cara gaped at her usually staid friend, who waggled a finger at her. "Don't look at me like that. I just wrapped up one set of my Ph.D. exams and haven't even been on a date for months. The only men I've had any contact with are my happily married academic advisor and a couple fellow students who either want to rip off my work or discuss the Freudenthal suspension theorem in loving detail. So I deserve a little personal time with a man who has more to offer than his perspective on advanced mathematics."

"If that's what you want, you won't have any trouble. Like Demetria said, Greek guys love blond Americans." Several of the men on the beach, accompanied or not, had noticed Emma reclining on her towel, her bikini a perfect foil for her creamy skin.

"Thanks for the vote of confidence, but what about you, Cara? Not that you're unlucky in love—who hasn't been?"

Cara muffled an ironic snort. Calling her unlucky in love was like calling the *Titanic* unlucky in seaworthiness.

Emma lifted her sunglasses and looked around. "But Aphrodisias certainly has a nice crop of men. If you don't find one you like, wait for the next ferry to bring another. And when he leaves, look for a different one. We have the whole summer."

Cara was momentarily speechless at her friend's logical approach, and couldn't help but tease her. "And if we don't find suitable men here," Cara went on, "we could always hop the ferry over to Naxos or Paros and search there. Or would leaving the island negate the Aphrodite Effect?"

Emma scoffed. "You're still not getting into this place, are you?"

Cara shifted and rested her head on her arms so Emma couldn't see her expression. "It's lovely, and I don't mean to rain on your vacation."

"So don't. You've needed to unwind ever since we've met, and this is your chance. Come fall, it's back to the salt mines."

Cara couldn't disagree. She was signed up for a full course load, leaving no time for even thoughts of hot beaches and hotter men. "We'll see about the men." Maybe a nice, calm Brit or German would pass through to do a spot of bird-watching or nature photography. She could dip her toe in the water with a guy named Graham or Klaus.

"Although if you're going to be lucky at love, you'll need a hotter swimsuit than that." Emma made a disparaging gesture at Cara's white terry cloth cover-up and perfectly serviceable black one-piece suit. "Put a skirt on that thing and you'd look like my grandma going to her water aerobics class."

Cara groaned. "Nice, very nice."

Emma stretched her arms over her head. "I think I've had enough sun for the first day. Like you said, I don't want to spend the summer crying on the couch from sun poisoning."

"Maybe you wouldn't have that problem with a swimsuit like mine." Cara couldn't resist the gibe.

"Smart off all you want, but we're going to the swimsuit shop on our way back to the villa." Emma sat up and reached for her shorts and sandals. "My treat."

"You don't need to pay for a swimsuit for me." Emma was a typical cash-strapped grad student.

Emma stood and brushed the sand off her limbs. "Consider it a thanks for this incredible summer vacation." She offered a hand up to Cara. "I insist."

Cara started to protest, but changed her mind. Emma had her pride, and Cara understood pride. After all, how much could a bikini cost?

"ONE HUNDRED twenty-five euros? Are you nuts?" Cara yanked at the spaghetti straps of the turquoise string bikini. On reflection, she shouldn't have been surprised. Any swimsuit store located half a block from a tourist beach was not going to be a bargain hunter's paradise.

Emma lightly slapped her hands away from the neck ties. "Come on, Cara, this suit looks amazing on you. The color makes your eyes as blue as the ocean—"

"And my skin as pale as the sand," Cara interjected.

"So you aren't tanned to the consistency of saddle leather. I'm telling you, this is the suit for you and I won't take no for an answer."

"But—"

"The proper response is 'thank you.'"

"Thank you, Emma."

Emma pulled her into a hug. "No, thank *you*. I'm going to look at that hot-pink bikini while you change." She left Cara in the small curtained changing room.

Cara studied her reflection. She couldn't remember the last time she'd examined herself closely in the mirror. Once upon a time, she had done practically everything but measure herself with calipers to see how fat she'd been. Which was to say, not fat at all.

And she still wasn't fat, despite how her former self would have fainted with horror to know how much weight Cara had gained over the past couple years.

Cara shook her head, glad to be past that craziness. Instead, she looked healthy. She pivoted to see her back in the mirror. Her butt looked full but not jiggly under the thin stretch material, and she even had a couple dimples at the base of her spine. She turned to see the front view and cupped her breasts to make sure the two triangles of fabric would be sufficient. Not that that really mattered since no one batted an eye at topless sunbathing. As she adjusted her breasts, her nipples tightened and poked against the fabric. She impulsively brushed one with her thumb and shuddered in pleasure. The suit was too tight, she should have realized. It rubbed all sorts of sensitive areas, her breasts, nipples, especially the strip between her legs.

"Cara? Are you ready?" Emma called. Cara started; she'd been about to slip her hand inside her suit bottom.

"Just a minute." She hurriedly changed back into her heavy black swimsuit and white terry cloth cover-up. They felt like a muumuu in comparison to the sexy blue bikini. She burst out of the curtained cubicle, suit in hand. "I'll take it."

"I'm paying, remember?" Emma plucked it away and set it on the counter in front of the young, dark-haired girl.

Cara turned to the salesclerk. "Do you have it in any other colors?"

Emma raised her eyebrows. "I told you it was a great suit."

The clerk ambled over to the racks and selected three suits—one black, one yellow, and the last a melon-orange. Emma shook her head at the yellow. "You'll look like your liver's acting up with that color. How about the black?"

"I like the melon color." Cara held it up in front of her.

"You look very nice in that color—most ladies not so much," the clerk offered.

"She's right, Cara. It's great with your hair and the gold trim on the cups and beads on the ties really make it shine."

Cara took the black one from the clerk, as well. "The blue, the black and the orange." She reached over to another rack. "And both of these crocheted cover-ups. I think the white one will look nice with the turquoise and the black with the black bikini, of course. And those three pairs of matching thong sandals in American size nine." The woman scurried around, gathering up Cara's selections. "Emma, what are you getting?"

Emma's eyes had widened. "Cara, are you sure you should get all this? We'll be here for longer than we planned moneywise."

Cara stopped for a second. "Really, Emma, don't worry about it. I built some shopping into my budget. You know how frugally I live."

Emma laughed and visibly relaxed. "Frugally is right. Some might even call it cheaply. But shopping spree or no, the blue suit's still on my bill."

"Agreed." But Cara noticed how Emma returned the hot-pink bikini that she'd been admiring to the rack.

Emma paid for the blue suit with a wad of euros and took the parcel. Cara caught the clerk's eye and gestured for her to pull that hot-pink suit back out. The woman nodded. "Emma, why don't you walk down to that café we passed and grab a sidewalk table for us? We should have an afternoon snack since dinner doesn't start until about nine or ten o'clock."

"You have a good idea," the clerk chimed in. "The outdoor tables are always busy and they have excellent pastries, as well."

"Sure!" Emma scooted out of the shop. She'd been eager to try different Greek desserts. Once she was gone, Cara quickly selected a matching cover-up and sandals for the hot-pink bikini. The total came to over six hundred euros, which Cara put on her platinum credit card without a second thought.

As the clerk was wrapping her purchases, a jewelry display under the glass countertop caught Cara's eye. Definitely beach jewelry—various ankle bracelets, toe rings and belly button rings. She stopped and touched her own navel. Her piercing was still open, although she almost never wore anything but a plain tiny silver ring.

"Would the lady like to see the jewelry? We have a gold-and-pink ankle bracelet that would look lovely with your friend's suit," the clerk offered.

Cara cursorily eyed the bracelet. "Fine, add the matching toe ring, as well." But she couldn't take her eyes off the belly button rings. "What about the light blue stone?" It was large and the same color as the afternoon Aegean sky.

"Very high quality. In Greek is *akouamarina*—water of the sea. In English, nearly the same."

"Aquamarine." A stone named after seawater was a perfect choice for an island summer. Almost…destiny? Cara dismissed the echo of Athena's words. "I'll take it, as well."

The clerk did a little half leap of joy but managed to restrain herself enough to tally up the second bill. Cara figured it was fitting to return some of her dough to the Greek economy, back from whence it came.

"You come back again, okay? You ask for me. My name is Niki, and I take good care of you."

"Thank you." Cara was royally ushered to the exit, where Niki held the door for her. The late-afternoon sun blasted her in the face, so she popped her hat and sunglasses back on.

The café Emma was waiting at was only about two or three blocks down the main road from the shop. Cara strolled down the sidewalk and walked in front of a narrow alleyway.

A screech of brakes made her stop dead in her tracks as a Vespa-type motor scooter skidded to a halt a foot from her legs. The sunglasses-wearing driver gave an angry shout in Greek that questioned her brains and skills of observance.

Cara fought the urge to tell him where to get off, using several pungent Greek verbs, and instead pulled her sunglasses off, giving the young, curly-haired guy her best freezing glare. "Why don't you look where you're going, you bonehead? Pulling out of an alley where you can't see who might be walking in front of you—where'd you learn how to drive—Apollonias?" She figured that might twist the knife a bit. Apollonias was the nearest island and Aphrodisias's fiercest rival for soccer matches and tourist dollars. She didn't know if he'd understand much of her English tirade, but it felt good to get it off her chest. When in Greece, do as the Greeks, and they hadn't been the silent, stoic type for several thousand years.

The guy's jaw dropped, and instead of continuing their insult-fest, he began to laugh. "Woo, watch out for those

American girls—they'll straighten you out anytime." He repeated his comment in Greek for the interested passersby, who all laughed.

Cara fought a smile, but the corners of her mouth must have given her away, because Vespa-Boy turned his charm in her direction. "And they don't hold grudges, either, do they? Come for coffee with me, beautiful blue-eyed girl. Everyone knows Americans are so friendly." He spoke English well, the hint of a Greek accent lending a sexy touch.

"I'm not *that* friendly," she retorted, ignoring the curl of awareness running down her spine. "Try running over an Italian girl—they go for that sort of thing."

He laughed again and adjusted his stance to balance the scooter. She couldn't help notice how his strong thighs straddled the narrow seat, the denim pulling across his zipper. "But will she be as clever as you?"

Cara gave him a pull-the-other-leg look. "A guy like you doesn't do cleverness."

He leaned close to her, close enough for her to see the black stubble along his hard jaw and smell the tang of sun and sweat. "You'd be surprised what I do. And who I do it with."

Wow. Suddenly her staid one-piece suit was rubbing the same places as the racy turquoise bikini had. She licked her suddenly dry lips, her face reflected in the lenses of his sunglasses. Vespa-Boy's nostrils flared, picking up on her unexpected response.

He started to say something, but another scooter came up the alley behind him and the driver shouted for him to get out of the way. "I'll see you around, clever American." He made it a promise and zoomed past her.

Cara exhaled noisily and walked toward the café, mentally scolding herself. She was here to help Athena and take a break after her first year of college, not boink the first guy who had floated her boat in years.

Emma caught sight of her and waved from the café. Cara made her way through the maze of tables and set down her packages. "Good, you went ahead and ordered." An assortment of desserts crowded the small table.

"I just pointed at a bunch of items on the menu and told the waiter to bring coffee, too. You'll have to tell me what these all are."

Glad for the distraction, Cara fell into tourist guide mode. "That custard with phyllo dough is *galaktobouriko,* the almond nut cake is *amygdalopita,* various cookies and the ubiquitous baklava." She leaned over the table. "Purists insist baklava has Turkish roots, but the last person who claimed that out loud was run out of Greece."

Emma laughed, drawing the admiration of the young waiter who'd just arrived with their coffee. He bowed. "Enjoy your sweets. I am at your disposal." He tossed a meaningful look at Emma, who just smiled.

"A possibility," she said, once he'd departed.

"A possibility for what?" Cara made a face. "He's probably seventeen years old."

"True," Emma agreed. "I don't want to find out the hard way the Greek penalties for fooling around with minors."

"Believe me, you won't have any trouble finding men who are old enough to stay up past curfew." Cara shoved the passing thought of reckless motorscooter drivers out of her mind and remembered her plan for finding an even-tempered Northern European type to test the waters with. No drama kings for her.

She spotted a possibility of her own and leaned over the table to Emma. "Emma, do you see that blond guy a few tables away?"

Emma casually turned as if she were watching people passing by and turned back. "That guy? The one wearing the hemp-looking Peruvian hoodie and sandals?"

"Emma, it is perfectly acceptable for European men to wear sandals."

"With woolen hiking socks?" Emma didn't wait for a response, mostly because there wasn't one Cara could think of. She gestured broadly. "All these Greek guys dying to meet American women and you're looking at some yahoo who probably has five pairs of lederhosen and yodels on the weekend?"

"Maybe Greek men aren't all they're cracked up to be."

"And maybe we should conduct a scientific sampling of the population to prove or disprove your hypothesis."

Cara lifted her hands in surrender. "Fine, sample away."

"I intend to." Emma broke off a chunk of nut cake and passed it to her. "Eat up. We're going out tonight, and you need your strength."

Cara accepted the cake and washed it down with her superstrong coffee. She flagged down the teenage waiter for another pot. She'd need the caffeine to keep up with Emma.

CARA HAD JUST FINISHED her shower and was toweling her hair dry in the bathroom when Emma knocked on the door. "Your cell phone's ringing."

"Oh, could you get it out of my purse and see who's calling?" Only a handful of people had her number and they wouldn't call just to chitchat. She hoped it wasn't her brother, Rick, calling with bad news about their grandmother, who was elderly and a bit senile.

Cara grabbed her terry cloth robe and wrapped herself in it, following Emma into the living room.

Emma handed her the phone. "It's a credit card company."

She sat down on the sectional couch and answered, "Hello?" After answering a multitude of security questions, she assured them she was indeed on a Greek island and likely to make even more purchases with her card. "What's my credit limit?"

She listened to the six-figure amount without blinking. "That should be fine." She had more than enough in her money market accounts to cover her purchases, short of buying the entire island.

Emma was watching her closely throughout her phone conversation. Cara hung up and wasn't surprised when Emma burst into questions. "Did you go over your card limit with all those suits? Do you need me to loan you some money?"

"No, no, I'm good, really—"

Emma paced back and forth over the marble floor. "Oh my gosh, Cara, I don't want you to go broke on this trip. I know we're both strapped for cash, and this trip out here must be costing you a fortune. Oh, I am so thoughtless. I have my teaching fellowship and living stipend, and you don't have any scholarships at the university."

"Emma, Emma, wait." Cara held up her hands and her friend finally stopped. "Come sit with me, Emma. It's okay."

Emma plopped down on the couch next to her. Cara thought for a second, considering the best way to alleviate her friend's worries. "Before I started college, I was married for a few years."

Whatever her friend was expecting, it obviously wasn't a confession of matrimony. "Cara, you were married? You never mentioned that before."

"It turned out not to be a good fit." That was the understatement of the century. "My husband was a bit older than I was and pretty set in his ways. I was young and naive and didn't realize he and I were looking for different things from life." Con had wanted a baby-maker, and she had wanted a faithful husband.

"Oh, wow." Emma's brown eyes widened. "Married. I just can't imagine it. Where did you live?"

"We had a condo in Chicago." Her brother had lived there for a brief time and then put it on the market for her when he moved out and got married. That alone had brought her a significant dollar amount. "When my marriage ended, I got a pretty good financial settlement, enough to send me back to school and allow for occasional trips."

"Your ex, do you see him anymore?"

"No, never." Cara heaved a sigh despite herself.

Emma must have picked up on her melancholy mood, because Cara found herself enveloped in a bear hug. "Thanks for telling me, Cara. I won't worry about you moneywise anymore."

Cara realized her lip was trembling. Aside from a couple people sworn to secrecy, she hadn't told anyone that her supposedly fairy-tale marriage was straight out of the legends of the Greek Furies. "Believe me, money is not a problem." She forced her expression into a determinedly cheerful one.

"Let's list what you *do* need. Fabulous summer in Greece—check. Hot bikinis and great beach to wear them on—check. Sexy Greek boy toy to give the beach and bikinis a workout—nope, you need to add him to your list."

"Back to the men again." But Cara giggled, encouraging Emma to continue.

"Back to the men, front to the men, sideways to the men—any way you like to the men. Now go get dressed. Like that weaving of Artemis above the couch, we're man-hunting tonight."

3

"THIS ONE." CARA STOPPED in front of a taverna around the corner from the main drag.

Emma looked at the unprepossessing building. "Are you sure?"

"Absolutely. You wanted authentic Greek island culture, this is it. No neon signs, no two-for-one drink specials or limbo contests." She hooked her arm through Emma's and drew her inside.

Once the cloud of cigarette smoke around her face disappeared, Cara saw several small tables and booths set around a dance floor. Piped-in Greek pop music came over the speakers. Cara pointed out a hand-lettered sign. "Looks like the live music starts in a half hour. Let's get a drink and grab a table before they fill up."

"Great." Now that they had a plan, Emma made her way to the bar and ordered a white wine for herself and red for Cara. Cara waved to her from the corner booth she'd claimed.

"Now what?" Emma asked after a few sips.

Cara shrugged. "Toss your hair, cast a few meaningful looks around the room. I suppose you could lick your lips seductively, but that might be a bit obvious." Just as she had licked her lips for Vespa-Boy.

"Not that. Besides, I think my outfit takes care of the obvious part." Cara had to agree. Emma wore a low-cut white halter top with a matching miniskirt and backless white shoes with a kitten heel. "Not to belabor the point, Cara, but maybe you should go to another of these boutiques for a more fun dress."

"You think this dress isn't fun?" Cara put on a hurt look, but burst into laughter at Emma's worried face. "Okay, okay, maybe this isn't the fanciest dress ever." That was an understatement. Her dress was a sleeveless black tunic with no discernible waistline, and she wore the same plain sandals she'd worn to the beach.

"There have to be some clothing boutiques around here. You need something that doesn't come from the sackcloth-and-ashes store. It's not like you're one of these Greek widows." Emma checked around the taverna and sipped her wine.

Cara blinked a couple times and looked down at her dress. Sew some sleeves on it, and she *would* look like an elderly widow. Many of them wore black for the rest of their lives after their husbands died. Athena did most of the time, and Athena's mother had worn nothing but black, if Cara remembered correctly. But they were decades older than she was—Athena in her seventies and her mother had pushed one hundred.

Although Cara felt ancient sometimes, she was only twenty-eight. Too young to dress in widow's clothing. "Emma?"

"Hmmm?" Her friend pulled her attention away from where the band was setting up.

"Do I wear a lot of black?"

"Aside from that dress and your one-piece swimsuit?"

Cara'd forgotten about her old-lady suit, but that was proving Emma's point. "I mean in general. Like back home in Michigan."

Emma furrowed her brow. "Come to think of it, you do. It's nice black clothing, like your cashmere turtleneck you loaned me and that really warm, long, wool skirt, but yeah, lots of your wardrobe is black."

"I had no idea." Cara mentally sorted through her closet at home. Aside from some warm-weather T-shirts and shorts, she did have a ton of black clothes.

"You look great in black, Cara," her friend reassured her. "It's a very cosmopolitan look, almost European."

Oh, boy. She'd been dressing in widow's weeds, to coin a British phrase from one of her literature classes. Mourning her marriage? Atoning for its painful ending? She knew Con wouldn't have wasted any time on regrets or recriminations, especially since he had considered everything to be all her fault.

Suddenly, her shapeless clothing offended her. Why should Con have any more say in what she wore? "Emma, this dress sucks."

Emma choked on her wine, sputtering a couple drops on her sleek white outfit. Cara passed her a cocktail napkin. "Oh my gosh, Cara," she said after regaining her ability to talk. "You shouldn't startle me like that. Good thing I'm not drinking red wine."

"But you agree."

"Well…not in so many words, but yes, it could do with a good bonfire."

Cara laughed. "How about my old black one-piece swimsuit?"

"That, too. But it has so much padding and synthetic stretch fabric I think we might get arrested for air pollution if we did try to burn it." Emma drummed her fingers on the table. "How about we throw it all away and start fresh? Not to be indelicate, but your lingerie could use some spiffing up, as well."

"It's a plan." She'd stop in the swimsuit boutique tomorrow and ask that clerk Niki about the best places to shop. She drained her wineglass and set it down. "You want another glass of wine, Emma?"

"That would be great."

Cara's trip to and from the bar took a bit longer than before. The place was starting to fill up with mostly locals as far as she could tell. Cara knew she stood out as an obvious foreigner, but no one paid her much attention aside from a few stares from the men. They'd need X-ray vision tonight to guess what her body looked like.

Cara turned the corner and stopped. Their cozy booth had just become a bit cozier. Emma was sitting between two Greek guys, her blond hair in stark contrast with their black. Unsure if her friend had invited them to sit or if they needed running off, Cara approached cautiously.

Emma spotted her. "There you are! Come meet Nick." She gestured to the man practically sitting in her lap, a guy with short black hair and dark brown eyes. "And this is his friend…" She was having trouble with the second guy's name, so he supplied it.

"Yannis." He turned to look at Cara. Despite his lack of sunglasses, the poor lighting and the fact that he wasn't straddling a scooter in tight jeans, Cara recognized him right away. Vespa-Boy. And he had the bluest, bluest eyes she'd ever seen. Wow. Good thing he'd kept his sunglasses on while they argued that afternoon, or else she might have licked more than just her lips.

"Yannis! I knew it was something like that. What is that in English?" Emma giggled. Cara reluctantly set her white wine down in front of her. Emma didn't have much alcohol tolerance.

"John," Cara and Yannis answered simultaneously and looked at each other.

He smiled slowly. "You speak Greek?"

"Not really," Cara fibbed. Fortunately Nick was doing his best to charm Emma so she wasn't paying attention.

"A clever American girl like you should be able to pick up Greek during your stay. I'll teach you some if you sit with me." Yannis gestured to the small slice of booth next to him. She'd practically have to sit in the guy's lap to avoid falling on the floor, which was probably the whole idea. And a bad idea. Right? A very bad idea.

"I'm afraid I need more room than that."

He looked disappointed but gave her more space. She sat cautiously and sipped her wine, unsure of what to do next.

Yannis had no uncertainties. "You never did tell me your name."

She swallowed her wine. "Cara."

"Cara? Just Cara?"

"Cara Sokol."

"And I am Yannis Petrides. Born on Aphrodisias, grew up here—I even learned how to drive here. *Not* on Apollonias." He lifted one black eyebrow in amusement.

Cara burst into laughter, remembering her insult regarding his driving skills.

"Ah, much better, Cara Sokol. I am sorry I almost ran you down today. All I can say is that your beauty stunned me so much I forgot how to stop my scooter."

She laughed even harder. "Oh, come on. In that outfit I could have been your grandma."

"My grandmother doesn't have eyes blue as the sea or hair as red as the sun when it drops into the ocean." He didn't touch her with anything but his words and his gaze, but that was more than enough.

Again at a loss, Cara glanced away. Really, she needed to get a grip. She was no blushing virgin ready to fall at the feet of a smooth-talking Greek charmer. And please, just because his blue eyes sparkled in his handsome bronzed face was no reason to go all stupid over the man. He was probably a total dud in bed.

After all, who wanted to sleep with a guy whose shoulders were wide from some kind of manual labor, whose hard thigh had pressed on hers, whose strong forearms would be more than able to hold his weight as he moved on top of her…. She drank more wine. "Oh, my, looks like I drank it all. I'll just go get a refill." She needed to catch her breath and stood, but he came out of the booth right after her.

He plucked her empty glass from her hand, his firm, callused fingers brushing hers. His white, straight teeth flashed in the dim light, his lips perfectly curved around them. "And what kind of Aphrodisian would I be if I let a lovely visitor get her own wine?"

For a split second, Cara thought he had said *aphrodisiac*. Oh, yes, Yannis Petrides was a potent aphrodisiac for her, judging from how her breathing had sped up and her nipples had tightened under the baggy black linen dress. She tossed a look Emma's way, but she was engrossed in dark-eyed Nick.

Yannis seemed to pick up on her nervousness. "Will you still be here when I come back with your wine, Cara?" he asked quietly. "Or will you run like a frightened maiden from the pursuits of the Old Ones?"

He meant like the girls who tried to escape the amorous attentions of Apollo and Zeus in Greek mythology. Cara tipped her chin up at him. "Why? Are you going to turn me into a tree if I don't return your attentions?"

He grinned again. "Ah, very good. You do know our stories."

"Since I didn't see Apollo's sun-chariot parked outside the taverna, I think I'm safe. And I don't run." At least not anymore.

"Good. Although if you spend much time here, you'll find Greek men enjoy the chase."

"But do you know what to do once you've caught your prey?" she retorted, annoyed yet aroused at the idea of him chasing her.

Yannis gave her a long sweeping look from her feet to her rapidly heating face. "I can't say for other men, but yes, *I* definitely do."

YANNIS BLEW OUT a long breath as he stood at the bar waiting for Cara's red wine. He'd planned to go out for a few drinks with his old friend Niko Theodoridis, listen to some live music, and maybe talk about the latest football matches. But he'd never expected to meet the girl he'd almost run down earlier. He felt a bit guilty, speeding down a narrow alley and then shouting at her for not paying attention. She hadn't understood his Greek, but had sure understood his message, giving it back to him in full measure.

He grinned. When he'd seen her beautiful blue eyes and the fiery red hair poking out from her ugly beach hat, she could have called him the son of a motherless goat and he would have just stood there and nodded.

Why was redheaded Cara here and not at an obnoxious tourist bar? Niko had tried to convince him to go to one of them since Niko had a thing for blondes, but Yannis had not wanted the lights and noise tonight.

Not to say he hadn't planned to find Cara. He had seen her shopping bag from the store where his cousin Niki worked and would have asked Niki about her tomorrow.

"Yannis!" Niko thumped him on the shoulder and ordered two white wines, what the blond girl had been drinking. While the bartender poured, Niko leaned his back on the bar and rested his elbows on top. "You're a great friend, man." His grin spread from ear to ear.

"What for?"

"For picking such a great place tonight."

They'd both been there dozens of times. "Glad I could find you your blond girl." Not really. Niko put too much store in looks. "It's been, what? A couple weeks since the last?"

"Yeah, Monika went back to Sweden in May. I've been lonely ever since."

Yannis shrugged. Niko liked the tourist girls because one, they left for home before things got awkward; two, they weren't related to him as half the girls on Aphrodisias were; and three, his mother was certainly not going to pressure him to marry some foreigner from Scandinavia, Great Britain, or God forbid, America.

The bartender passed them the wineglasses, and the men paid. Niko took a sip from his white and grimaced. "Give me a beer anytime."

"So get a beer." That actually sounded good to Yannis, so he ordered one.

Niko shook his head. "No, the girls like it if you drink the same thing they are. Makes you look more compatible."

"Whatever." Yannis reached into his pocket to pay for his beer, but Niko tossed some euros on the bar.

"This one's on me—as a thanks for distracting that redhead so I can get a little alone time with Emma."

"What?" Yannis set his bottle down on the bar with a decided thunk. "You think I'm talking with her as a favor to you?"

"Why else? It's not like you can see her body under that awful dress, and her hair's so red and pulled into that braid thingie." Niko made a face.

Well, if Niko couldn't see anything but blatant charms, Yannis wasn't about to point out the generous curves of Cara's breasts and hips that even that dress couldn't hide. And as for her hair…it *was* the color of the sun as it set over the western coast. Loose, it would drape over her pale shoulders like the painting of Aphrodite rising from the sea that he'd seen on a trip to Florence.

Yannis picked up his beer and Cara's wine. "Let's get back to the ladies, shall we? They might think we've ditched them and left."

Niko's look of alarm was almost amusing enough to distract him from his lustful thoughts of Cara. Almost, but not quite.

"Wow, Cara, you really picked a great place tonight." Emma had stars in her eyes. "This Nick guy is so-o-o-o cute."

"Great." This was not what Cara had planned. None of it. Vespa-Boy had a name—Yannis Petrides.

Cara listened halfheartedly while Emma chattered about Nick's manly charms. "Don't you think that sounds fun, Cara?"

"What?" Cara dragged her thoughts away from Yannis and focused on her friend.

"Double-dating. Maybe if tonight goes well, we can go out with Nick and his friend again. Nick seems fun, and Ya—Ya—"

"Yannis," Cara supplied.

"Whatever his name is, he sure seems into you." Emma giggled. "With him around, you can forget about that hippie hiker you were eyeing earlier."

Cara fought the urge to tell her that Greek men wore sandals, too, and usually despite extremely hairy feet, as well. "I just don't want to get involved with a Greek guy, Emma. They have the home field advantage, and they don't go home at the end of the week. I'd rather not spend the rest of the summer ducking down alleys to avoid running into the guy again. Too awkward."

Emma waved a hand negligently. "Who cares? Move on to the next guy."

Cara shook her head. Emma just didn't understand how a small Greek island worked. "All these guys grew up together and half of them are related to each other. It would be like dumping a guy and then dating his brother or cousin."

"*I'm* the one going home at the end of the summer, so who cares what the guys think? Besides, if Nick turns out to be as hot as I think he is, I won't need to look any further."

"As long as you have a plan," Cara commented drily.

"You should seriously consider following the same plan. What happens on Aphrodisias stays on Aphrodisias. Oh, look, here they come."

Cara hadn't needed Emma to tell *her* that. Her guy-dar had gone off as soon as Yannis was within ten feet of her.

He slid in the booth next to her. "Your wine, *despinis*," he announced with the suavity of an experienced waiter. Across the table, Nick delivered a white wine to Emma.

Cute. He'd called her miss. "Thank you." Cara took several sips while she thought of something to say. "This wine isn't what I had before."

"You like it? It's one of the island's vintages. The bartender usually saves it for the locals."

Cara could already feel its headier buzz rushing through her veins and wondered if he was trying to get her tipsy. "I guess it's okay." She felt as if she'd kicked a puppy when Yannis's face fell. "Well, you must not like it, since you're drinking a beer."

"I like it fine. My grandfather makes it from his vineyard." His sentences were short and clipped.

"Oh." Well, that certainly was an uncomfortable exchange. She toyed with the stem of her wineglass and looked anywhere but at Yannis.

Her gaze fell on Emma. Her alcohol intolerance was kicking in, and she gave a big yawn before snuggling on Nick's shoulder.

Cara needed to draw this evening to a close. "Emma, time to go." Her friend blinked a couple times and then shut her eyes.

"What?" Nick protested. "We just got here. The dancing hasn't even started." He wrapped an arm around Emma's shoulders.

"We also just got here from overseas. Emma's barely conscious thanks to the booze and jet lag." Cara tugged her friend out from under his overfriendly embrace. "Besides, Greek men can dance with each other. You two should go for a spin."

Nick gave her a blank look, but Yannis snorted and replied to his friend in Greek, "Look, Niko, they obviously don't want to hang around with us."

"But the blonde does—"

"Her friend's right. She's almost passed out. What fun is that?"

Cara broke in then, "Excuse me, please, Yannis." She

scooted into him, and her hip pressed along his. The long muscles of his thigh flexed at the contact, and she felt an answering pull. "Yannis?"

He shook his head and stood, letting her slide free. Emma fussed a bit, but straggled after her.

"You sure you can get her back to your hotel?" Yannis asked. "We can walk with you." Nick was pouting into his wineglass and didn't bother seconding Yannis's offer.

"No, thanks. We're not far." Cara tugged Emma's elbow.

"Nick, we're at the Aphrodite Bay Villas, Apartment Three," Emma announced loudly, unfortunately not drunk enough to forget their hotel information. "Call me."

Nick raised his head and a grin erased his sulky expression. "How do you Americans say it? Oh, yes. Count on it."

Probably too far into the busy season to find another hotel. Oh, well, Emma was a big girl, and hell-bent on getting her Greek groove on. In the meantime, Cara would try for a handsome tourist who'd be off to another island once the ferry arrived.

"Good night, then." Yannis gave her a curt nod and sat next to Nick. He reached for her wine and raised it mockingly. *"Yia sou."* He toasted her and drained the glass dry. "Ah, delicious. I'll have to tell my *pappous* what a good job he did on this vintage. There's a good reason we save it for ourselves and don't waste it on tourists."

She spun on her heel but forgot she was still holding onto Emma, who teetered dangerously on her flimsy shoes. Emma threw her arms around Cara's shoulders for balance and Cara staggered a bit under the weight. "Come on, Em, straighten up," she muttered, peeling Emma off her.

"Eh, it's okay here for women to dance together, too, but most of them wait for the music," Yannis called.

Cara tossed him a nasty glance and stalked off. The

dignity of their exit was ruined, however, by Emma blowing a kiss to the men and giggling again.

Cara finally got them out the door into the warm Grecian night and steered Emma uphill to their villa.

"Cara, the blue-eyed guy likes you! Could be something special."

Cara groaned. Since meeting Yannis Petrides for the very first time less than eight hours ago, he had almost run her down, she had chewed him out on the street, he had tried to get her tipsy and she had insulted his beloved grandfather's wine. *Special* wasn't the word that came to mind, but the other words that did would shock even a drunken Emma.

4

"So how was your evening out with Niko Theodoridis?" Yannis's aunt Eleni poured him a cup of coffee and set plates of hard-boiled eggs, olives and thick slices of homemade bread on the table in front of him.

"Eh, all right. I had some of *Pappous*'s wine at the taverna."

"Must not have been too much, or else you wouldn't have found your way home. Your uncle uses that wine to clean tarnished brass sometimes. It works like a charm."

It sure hadn't charmed a certain Cara Sokol. Ah, well. The ferry that brought her would take her away soon enough.

"Eat, eat!" his aunt urged. "A big handsome boy like yourself needs good food, especially to work construction for your slave driver uncle."

Yannis helped himself to the eggs and olives and drizzled local wild honey on the bread. He smiled up at *Theia* Eleni after a couple mouthfuls. "It's as delicious as you are beautiful."

She beamed down at him and patted her carefully combed and sprayed black hair. He'd seen her only once with her face bare and her hair limp and wet around her shoulders and had for a split second wondered if his uncle had sneaked a girlfriend into the house. "Oh, you! Your mother warned me you were a charmer. Like I told you before, my friend Georgia has a daughter who would be perfect for you. Just let me know if you want to meet her. Such a nice girl and a good cook." His aunt pinched his cheek and bustled back to the stove.

Yannis winced. Most of his aunt's friends were on the lookout for a husband for their girls, but he wasn't interested in girls in their late teens who only giggled when he tried to talk about more than the weather.

His uncle Gus came into the kitchen, still buckling his belt. Uncle Gus was wearing one of his dressier shirts today, a button-down white linen with embroidered panels down the chest over black dress pants. He must not be planning to visit a job site today. He sat and gestured to the empty table in front of him. "Coffee." Yannis's aunt quickly filled his cup and set down an ashtray, as well.

Yannis took a deep breath of the last clear air of the morning. Sure enough, his uncle lit a cigarette to smoke while drinking his coffee. Having grown up in Greece, Yannis was used to cigarette smoke, but didn't care for it at meals, where it seemed to change the flavor of his food.

He popped a couple more olives into his mouth and pushed the bowl toward Uncle Gus who raised a work-roughened hand in refusal.

"None for me. Time to go to work, anyway." He stubbed out his cigarette and stood. Yannis followed, his aunt fluttering after them with a couple bundles of pastries for their *kolatsio,* or midmorning snack. Yannis's uncle more than made up for missing breakfast then.

"Have a good day! I'm making lamb for dinner tonight." Aunt Eleni waved goodbye and then went back into the house, presumably to do whatever Greek women did all day at home.

"Lamb, eh?" Uncle Gus grinned at him as they hopped in his white compact car and backed out of the driveway. "And not even your name day for another couple weeks."

Yannis grinned. His name day was June 24, the birthday feast, or Nativity, of Agios Ioannis Prodomos, St. John the Baptist. Yannis's own birthday was in September, but name day feasts were celebrated more than birthdays, especially on an island where at least a quarter of the men were named some version of Ioannis.

"Ah, well, your aunt loves to have somebody else around to cook for since the girls are off in Athens." He lit another cigarette. "Up to no good there, I'm sure. But they won those islander scholarships to university and were on the next ferry out."

Yannis rolled down his window to let the ocean breeze blow through the car and privately thought his two cousins Marina and Petra had done well to get their education. Aside from tourism, fishing and small-scale farming, Aphrodisias didn't have many career opportunities. "Athens isn't as pretty as here. I'm sure they miss the island."

Uncle Gus grunted. "Probably marry boys from the mainland and only come back once a year."

Yannis nodded. That was a real possibility. Marina and Petra were related to half the guys on Aphrodisias and knew the other half too well to ever want to marry them. His uncle finished his cigarette and stubbed it out in the car's full ashtray. The island was too dry during the summer to flick butts out the window. Nobody wanted a brushfire, especially his uncle, who was in the middle of several building projects. "What's the plan for today, Uncle Gus?"

"You go over to the villa site and make sure those lazy bastards who call themselves finish carpenters are doing the door and window moldings correctly. The buyers are Germans and they'll come in with magnifying glasses and rulers to make sure everything's square." Uncle Gus would take foreigners' money for building houses, but that didn't mean he approved of them moving to Aphrodisias.

"Sure thing, Uncle."

"After our *kolatsio,* get them working again and then come back to the office. I want you to sit in on a meeting with some Belgian property investors. They're brand-new to the island and I don't want them to sign a contract with my competitors."

That would explain his uncle's dressier clothes. Yannis looked down at his own light blue T-shirt, well-worn jeans and steel-toed brown construction boots. "Should I change before the meeting?"

Uncle Gus made a dismissive gesture. "No. Let them see we are real working men who are not afraid to get dirty."

Yannis wasn't sure he wanted to be the poster boy for dirty working men, but he wasn't the boss. "What property is this about?"

His uncle pulled into a small parking spot in the alley behind his office and got out of the car. Yannis grabbed his tool belt out of the trunk. "One we don't have yet. *Kyria* Nomikou was about to sell it to Athena Kefalas for some weaving museum, but *Kyria* Nomikou just died a couple days ago, before any papers were signed. Her nephew from Athens is asking around to see if he can get a better price— maybe he can, if these Belgians are interested in building their villa condominiums there. If we can help arrange the real estate, they are interested in contracting us for the build." His uncle tipped him a wink as he unlocked the office door. "Now take a truck to the site, but—" he held up a hand "—park behind the trees where they can't see you and sneak up on them."

Yannis laughed. Sneaking up on men while he wore heavy boots and a bulky, noisy tool belt would be quite a feat. "Just how lazy are these carpenters?"

"Eh, they're from Apollonias. They think they're the sun god himself and the world revolves around them." His uncle tossed him one of the pastry bundles. "Bribe them with your aunt's baking if you have to. Those German buyers are coming next week and I need them to release the rest of the construction money—they won't, not unless everything is perfect. And don't forget to come back for the meeting."

"Okay, Uncle." Yannis stowed his gear in the battered Aphrodisias Builders pickup truck and hopped behind the wheel. The engine roared to life with a cloud of black exhaust. He pulled away and shook his head. So much for sneaking up on the lazy Apollonian carpenters—they'd hear and smell the truck a mile away.

"Wake up, sleepyhead, it's shopping time!"

Cara cracked open an eyelid and squinted up at the giant lemon sitting on her bed. She peeled open the other eye and realized it was Emma wearing a yellow T-shirt and matching shorts, her blond hair fluffed around her face. "Why am I feeling the wine and you aren't? You were a riot to get home last night."

"First, I seem to remember you made me drink a lot of water and take some aspirin before I fell asleep. Second, white wine makes you less hungover than red."

Cara grunted. She'd had several disturbing dreams featuring Yannis Petrides that had left her tossing and achy with need. Probably jet lag thrown in on top of it, too. "What time is it?"

Emma checked Cara's bedside clock-radio. "Ten o'clock."

"Good. Just in time for *kolatsio*." Cara sat up in bed, the sheet falling away from the oversize T-shirt she customarily wore to bed.

Emma grimaced. "What's with the big duck on that shirt?"

"It's comfortable." The caption below read, I'm on the Verge of a Quack-up, which had appealed to Cara's dark sense of humor a couple years back.

"Maybe we can give it to the housekeeper for her cleaning supplies. Don't be surprised if it mysteriously disappears. Even that hempy hippie you were eyeing yesterday would turn up his nose at it."

"But I sleep well when I wear it."

"Who said anything about sleep?" Emma winked at her and stood up. "I'll run to the bakery downstairs and get some breakfast. What sounds good?"

"Oh, get me a *bougatsa*—that's a baked phyllo pastry with sweet cheese if they have any fresh ones. Otherwise, whatever looks good."

"It *all* looks good to me. How do you want your coffee?"

"Black. I don't need the sugar and cream calories," she replied automatically.

Emma laughed. "Cara, you dingbat. You want me to get you a cheese-stuffed pie-thingie and you're worried about a packet of sugar and a drop of cream?"

Cara took a deep breath. Emma was right. As long as Cara walked or swam every day and didn't eat only *bougatsa,* she would be fine. "Okay, cream and sugar both." She liked her coffee a bit lighter and sweeter thanks to the strong brewing customs.

"That's more like it. And don't worry, I have no intention of letting you sit on your heinie on the beach all day. Have I mentioned we're going shopping?"

"Only about ten times," Cara replied drily. "Now be off with you and don't come back without my food."

"Yes, ma'am!" Emma saluted briskly and hurried out the door.

Cara hopped out of bed and looked down at her night-shirt. "No more quack-ups—or crack-ups, either." She stripped off the shirt and dropped it into the wastebasket.

By the time she'd finished her shower and wrestled her hair into submission, Emma was setting up breakfast on the terrace table.

"These cheese pastries are fresh out of the oven." Emma slid them onto bright blue-and-yellow plates from the villa kitchen and poured coffee from the foam containers into matching mugs. "Sit, sit."

Cara relaxed into one of the small wrought-iron chairs and dropped a napkin into her lap before slicing the pastry into flaky, gooey triangles. She forked one corner into her mouth and closed her eyes in ecstasy. "Oh, yum."

Emma sat down across from her and did the same. "Yum is right. Almost as delicious as that Nick guy from last night. I wonder if we'll run into him again?"

"Probably, since you gave him the address of our villa."

Emma hooted. "Did I? I don't remember that part, but I do remember his friend wasn't exactly hard on the eyes, either, judging from how you were looking at him."

Cara almost choked on her coffee. "How I was looking at him?"

"Yep, like he was the male equivalent of this pastry thingie." Emma wiggled her eyebrows and licked some cream filling off her fork.

"I have no idea what you're talking about." Cara tried

hiding her face behind the coffee cup, but Emma's laugh told her she'd been unsuccessful.

"Hey, no need to blush. I'm glad you've found a guy that piques your interest. There sure wasn't anybody back in Michigan, was there?"

"No, not at all." Cara had been asked out a few times, but had always declined due to her lack of interest. But being on Aphrodisias seemed to have flipped on some long-dormant libido switch.

But just because Yannis had featured prominently in her dreams last night didn't mean he was automatically her first choice for Chief Libido Fixer. After all, Cara was on an island. Surely, there were other fish in the sea.

"AND THEN SHE SAID, 'That's no goat, that's my mother!'" Uncle Gus delivered his punch line triumphantly as the Belgian real estate investors roared with laughter.

Yannis laughed along with them even though he'd heard it a million times.

His uncle caught his eye. "Eh, Yannis, fetch some of that red your *pappous* makes." He turned back to the Belgians. "My father-in-law makes this wonderful wine by hand up in the mountains. Stomps his own grapes and everything. Famous all over the island."

Famous for polishing tarnished metal and pissing off American girls. They were entertaining their foreign guests in the taverna around the corner from his uncle's office, the same taverna where he and Niko had run into the American girls last night.

Yannis leaned on the bar and placed his order for two bottles of red. Red wine for the redhead. Boy, had he read her wrong. Sure, she had a tart mouth on her, but he thought he could sweeten her up. A little local color, some homegrown spirits, but no luck. Maybe next time he'd try for a girl whom he hadn't almost run down in the street. Showed a lack of finesse, a modern version of clubbing her over the head and dragging her off to his cave.

But what a fun time they could have had together in a cave, her pale body shining up from a bed of furs, her red hair glowing in the light from a small fire, her full lips calling his name as he moved inside her... Yannis sighed and discreetly adjusted his tightening jeans.

The taverna owner, an old family friend, returned with the uncorked bottles. "Tell your grandfather I need another case. His stuff is a hit this summer."

"I'll be sure to let him know."

"And tell your uncle to have those foreigners sign his papers before they pass out."

Yannis grinned and thanked the bartender, his construction boots squeaking on the stone floor as he joined his uncle and their guests. If this deal went through, Yannis would be too busy to worry about what one prickly redhead thought of him anyway.

"WHEN ON EARTH did you get your belly button pierced?" Emma stared at Cara's navel in fascination as Cara took off her new beach cover-up and settled onto her beach towel. "I only left you for a few minutes to get breakfast."

"Silly." Cara laughed and applied sunblock with a heavy hand, careful to get the parts that her new turquoise bikini left bare. "I've had this for years. You've just never seen my stomach before."

"And that is a beautiful stone. Aquamarine?"

Cara nodded. "I thought it was appropriate for our island adventure. Oh, I almost forgot. I have a little something for you."

Emma frowned. "You already got me this fancy pink bikini when I was the one supposed to be treating you. It better be something cheap like a souvenir refrigerator magnet saying Welcome to Aphrodisias."

"Sorry. Although I suppose you could hang them on your fridge if you want." Cara reached into her tote bag and pulled out the box holding the ankle bracelet and toe ring she'd bought at the swim boutique yesterday.

Emma opened the box and squealed. "Oh my gosh, Cara! They're beautiful. I've never seen pink crystals like this."

Cara just smiled. They were actually pink topazes, but she didn't want to shock Emma's thrifty Midwestern side. "Try them on."

"If you insist." Emma giggled and clipped the bracelet on her ankle and slid the toe ring on the opposite foot.

"Whoo, sexy." Cara gave a wolf whistle as Emma admired the jewelry.

"Thank you so much, Cara." Emma smiled down at her feet, but turned a serious face to Cara. "Are you sure—" she dropped her voice to a whisper "—are you *absolutely* sure this present and this whole trip is not going to cause a money problem for you? I would just *die* if this was your tuition money you're spending on us."

Cara patted her shoulder. "Please don't worry. Athena got us a good deal on the villa and like I told you, I have money of my own." Actually it used to be Con's money, but he wasn't around to complain how she spent it.

"Okay." Emma's sunny expression returned. "But our evening out tonight is my treat."

"Oh, are we going out tonight?" Cara pulled her beach hat low over her eyes and lay back on the towel, the sun warming and relaxing her.

"Our first Friday night on vacation? Of course. I thought

we could go for dinner and dancing, and you can wear one of your new outfits. Maybe that jade-colored dress."

"Whatever you want." Cara yawned. Maybe she could catch a nap, hopefully one without dreams of that blue-eyed Yannis.

5

"YOU SET ME UP, EMMA!" Cara stopped dead in her tracks as she spotted the table her friend was aiming for.

Emma hooked her arm through Cara's elbow and tugged her through the dark, romantic restaurant toward where Nick Theodoridis waved to them, his buddy Yannis seated next to him. "Come on, Cara. Who else do we know on this island?"

"Athena, Demetria—"

"Who are very nice ladies, but not what I had in mind for a fun evening out. Now smile at the men."

Cara managed a small lip curl. Her only consolation was that Yannis seemed as surprised as she was.

"Ladies!" Nick called. Yannis stood as they approached the table, Nick hastily following his example.

Emma greeted the men and let Nick kiss her on the cheek. Cara stuck out her hand when he tried the same with her. He was Emma's problem.

Now for *her* problem, dressed in a silky-looking dark blue button-up shirt and black dress pants. "Hello, Yannis."

He didn't try to kiss her, only engulfed her hand with his. "Cara." Her name, combined with the warm, hard strength of his fingers made her a bit fuzzy, as if she'd been drinking his grandpa's homemade red. "Shall we sit?" he asked. "Emma told Niko to order for you ladies, so dinner should be here in a few minutes."

Realizing she still held his hand, she let go. "Oh. Sure." She found herself staring at his chest, a slender chain and small gold religious medal resting right below the warm hollow of his throat.

Emma was already absorbed in Nick, her blond head almost touching his dark one.

Cara sat, suddenly uncomfortable in her new clothes. She was wearing the jade dress she'd bought just that morning. The halter top left bare a revealing amount of her cleavage and shoulders. She wished she'd worn a wrap to the restaurant despite the warm room. She sneaked a glance sideways at Yannis, but he was staring ahead with an expression she couldn't read.

YANNIS HOPED the lovely Cara couldn't tell what was going through his mind. Probably not, since she'd be up and running away again if she knew a lightning bolt the size of Zeus had zapped him as soon as he saw her again.

He'd known she was hiding decent looks under her baggy outfit last night, but *gamoto!* He'd had no real idea. This dress was sleeveless, too, but other than that, they might as well have come from different planets. *This* dress had absolutely no back, which was sexy enough by itself, but then the top wrapped around the nape of her neck and squeezed her breasts together in the middle of her neckline.

Her breasts were full and pale, like the moon that shone over the sea, lightly sprinkled with golden freckles. He wanted to connect them with his tongue and then lick a line to her nipples.

He cleared his throat and she jumped. She was as on edge as he was. For the same reason? He couldn't tell. Across from them, the blonde giggled again, and this time she was drinking mineral water. Nick might get his wish tonight. Yannis wouldn't. But that was no excuse to be rude. "So, what do think of our island?"

She turned her face up to his and he swallowed hard. She'd left her hair long and loose and one red curl had trickled onto her breasts. He wanted to reach over to stroke her with it, but figured she'd slap him, and deservedly so.

"Aphrodisias is very nice," she replied politely. "The beach is nice, the views are nice and the sea is…"

"Nice?" he supplied, gratified at the hastily tamped-down flare of anger in her eyes.

"Something like that." She shifted away from him and sipped her mineral water.

He suppressed a sigh. "Where do you live in the States?" He picked up his wineglass, figuring he'd need a belt to get through this long evening.

"Michigan. A town called Ann Arbor."

The red burned its way down his windpipe. He choked for a minute while she thumped him on the back. "Ann Arbor? Isn't there a big university there?"

"University of Michigan. I go to school there." She furrowed her brows. "Have you ever been there?"

He could honestly say no and shook his head. Ohio State University, where he was finishing his master's degree in architecture, was several hours away from Ann Arbor and University of Michigan's fiercest sports rival. Not that he had any time for that. Grad school was brutal, and he was determined to do well.

Not that he'd tell her anything about his schooling. She didn't seem interested at all. Probably thought of him as some hearty Greek peasant, strong but stupid. "Is your friend a student, too?"

"Emma is one of the most brilliant young mathematicians in the country."

"Which country?" He couldn't help himself. Americans were fiercely territorial about having the best, being the best.

"Any country. She has one more year until she earns her doctorate in math and already has several top job offers—Cal Tech, Jet Propulsion Labs, even MIT wants her." She leaned in close, her blue eyes snapping. "Nothing or nobody should distract her from her degree. We are here for a relaxing summer, but that's it."

"You're here for the whole summer?" He didn't know whether to groan or cheer.

"The whole summer." Funny, she didn't look pleased at the idea.

"Won't you get bored?" He spoke without thinking. Just because he needed to be active didn't mean she was the same.

"Don't worry about me—I have plenty to do. Shopping, swimming, sunbathing."

Typical tourist stuff. But for a whole summer? "Sounds fun."

She widened her eyes in alarm. "I'm not fishing for you to take me around or anything." She gestured to Niko, who was whispering to her friend. "Whatever they get up to is their business."

"Oh. Sure." Why was he disappointed? He had plenty on his plate, especially now that the new investors had signed on the dotted line for the condo villas during their slightly drunken meeting. He had to help get that real estate deal for the actual property so he could tweak the designs.

The rest of dinner was a long, drawn-out affair. Niko couldn't stop hand-feeding the giggling blonde and Cara picked at her lemon chicken until he snapped.

"What's the matter? Don't you like Greek food?"

She looked at him, her big eyes even wider. "What?"

"Your dinner." He gestured at her barely touched plate. "You won't enjoy your summer on Aphrodisias if you don't eat."

"Oh." She stared down at the uneaten remains. "I think it's the cigarette smoke. People don't smoke nearly this much at home and it's giving me a headache."

Yannis nodded. Americans often complained about the smoky atmosphere. "You need to go back to your hotel?"

"Well…" Her gaze drifted over to Niko and her friend. "I don't want to ruin Emma's evening. She works very hard and this is her first vacation in years."

"Niko will look after her."

A spark of her previous spirit resurfaced. "I'm sure he will. But yes, I need some fresh air." She dropped her napkin on the table and slid out of the booth. "Emma, honey, the cigarettes are getting to me. I'm going to call it a night."

Emma dragged her attention away from Niko and focused on her friend. "Cara, you hardly ate anything. Are you feeling okay?"

"Fine, fine." She shrugged. "I thought I'd just walk back to our villa and see Aphrodisias at night."

Emma bit her lip and looked at Niko. "Is that safe?"

"Perfectly safe, *chriso mou*. That means 'my golden one,'" he added meaningfully.

"Oh, Nick," she sighed, her fingertips fluttering at his chest. He captured her hand and brought it to his lips to kiss.

Yannis rolled his eyes and saw Cara doing an eye roll to match. At least they agreed on something.

Then Niko gave him a pleading look. Yannis gave him a narrow stare back, but gave in and stood. "I'd be happy to take Cara back to your place if that would make you feel better."

"Not necessary," Cara clipped out. "No one's going to bother me."

Yannis wasn't so sure, judging from the interested looks she was getting just in the restaurant. And the way back to her villa passed by several raucous tourist bars.

"You know, Nick, we can always get together some other time," Emma offered, pulling her hand from his friend's grip.

Cara must have seen the other couple's disappointment, since she visibly softened. "Okay, Yannis, I'll take you up on your offer. Emma, you stay and enjoy yourself."

Niko quickly masked his triumph. "Cara, nice to see you again, and I hope you feel better soon. Emma, have you ever seen the sea by moonlight?"

Yannis took this as his cue to hustle Cara out the door before she could wreck Niko's grand plan. Cara walked in front of him, showing the long slender curve of her spine. He caught up to her near the bar where a group of people blocked her and put his hand on her back.

She stopped, startled. "Yannis?"

He fought down his reaction to her silky-smooth skin and instead steered her through the crowd. Once they were clear, though, he wasn't in any hurry to remove his hand.

They emerged into the warm night air and Cara took several deep breaths, forcing Yannis to drop his hand.

"Better?" he inquired.

"Much." She laughed, walking away and giving him a nice eyeful of how her hips swayed under the tight green skirt. "Can you believe I used to be a smoker?"

He followed her before she could catch him staring. "Really?" She didn't seem like the type.

"For four or five years. And now I can't stand to be around it for very long. When I first quit, I would purposely stand close to people smoking so I could breathe in some fumes. Secondhand smoke was better than nothing. Are you a smoker?"

"No, I never started. I must be the only Greek man on the island who doesn't smoke."

"I thought so—you smell really good."

"I do?"

"Well, not like stale smoke," she backpedaled, picking up her pace.

He sighed inwardly. Not willing to give an inch. They were almost back to her villa anyway. Cara suddenly slowed at the entrance to a discotheque, Greek pop music pulsing through the air.

"You like to dance?" he asked.

"Sometimes." She was tapping her toes, though, their red-painted nails peeking out through her sexy high-heeled shoes.

"Come on." He caught her elbow and guided her into the dark club, ignoring her protests. Time for him to be a stereotypical overbearing Greek male. "You want to dance, let's dance."

She was yelling at him and gesturing ferociously, almost like a native Greek. Fortunately, he couldn't hear her over the music and just shook his head and pointed at his ears.

She glared at him for a minute, but the heavy beat of the music was getting to her. He started moving his shoulders and she joined him, gradually relaxing enough to swing her hips in time to the beat. "That's it," he shouted. "You're a great dancer."

She relented and gave him a slight smile, raising her arms as she twirled in a tight circle on the crowded dance floor, colored lights flashing around them. Her breasts shifted under her thin halter, and he could swear he saw the edge of her puckered areola, waiting for *him,* Yannis Petrides, to free it from her dress and lavish attention on it. He hardened immediately as her dress gaped enough for him to see the beautiful slope of her breast, as well.

Gamoto! It was difficult to keep dancing in his aroused state. Cara did some shimmy-type moves and had turned her back to him when some drunk guy staggered by and knocked Yannis into her. He automatically wrapped his arm around her waist to keep her from falling. By some awkward coincidence, his cock rubbed her as she squirmed against him and then nestled him right between her curvy cheeks.

She froze as if in shock. He was about to apologize and explain, but groaned instead as she slowly began grinding her hips into him, her breath coming faster. His hand crept up from her waist, her heavy breast resting on his fingers. Only a few more inches to slip inside her top. It was dark there, and everybody was caressing each other in lustful abandon.

Then the music changed to Giorgios Mazonakis singing "Summer in Greece," a pop hit from a couple years ago that described foreign girls getting drunk on the beach and appreciating the sensual skills Greek men had to offer them.

She faced him, her breasts rubbing his chest. He smiled in satisfaction, and her easy expression stiffened. What now? Was it that stupid song? She jumped away from him and stalked out of the club. He considered not following her for a second.

Who was *she* to lead Yannis Petrides around like a pet goat on a string? He had no responsibility for her. He wasn't her brother, cousin, boyfriend *or* lover. Although the last…

"Gamoto!" He muttered a Greek curse and went after her. He'd promised to see her home, happily or not. And once she was there, she could stay there for the rest of the summer for all he cared.

WHY DID YANNIS have to give her that smile in the club? Just shy of a smirk, it told her, *I win and you lose.* And Cara was not about to lose anything else to a man. She'd lost enough.

She heard him following her, his breath loud and angry in the quiet streets nearing the villa. She reached the wrought-iron gate at the foot of the staircase leading up to her place and turned. His face was shadowed, but she could feel the tension radiating off him.

"Thanks for bringing me home, Yannis." Her tone meant the exact opposite.

"My pleasure, Cara." His tone was a match.

She unlocked the gate and passed through, acutely aware of his stare as she climbed the stairs. She rounded the corner onto the landing and his steps sounded, growing fainter and fainter.

But a noise was growing louder and louder as she approached the door to their villa. A kind of moaning, groaning sound.

Cara's shoulders slumped. She recognized that sound. Sure, it had been longer than she wanted to admit, but she knew the sounds of sex when she heard them.

Oh, crap. Emma and Nick must have rushed back to the villa as soon as Cara and Yannis left, passing them during their side trip into the nightclub.

Cara touched the doorknob, which turned under her grasp. Maybe Emma had managed to lure Nick as far as the bedroom, and Cara could steal some blankets and sleep on Athena's couch.

She peeked into the apartment and fought back her own groan. Apparently Nick's charm was such that they hadn't made it any farther than the rug in front of the couch. Fortunately Cara only saw Emma's legs wrapped around Nick's calves, but she had a full-on view of naked Nick's backside in all its hairy, thrusting glory.

Cara cringed and closed the door as carefully as avoiding a trip wire. So much for taking blankets—she'd use Athena's bath towels for bedding before interrupting *that* scene. She went back down the stairs and took the street that would eventually lead her back to Athena's.

"Hey, what are you doing?" a male voice called.

She jerked to a halt and cautiously looked around. Damn it, the stupid street was as dark as Hades, to coin a Greek simile. "Go away and leave me alone!" she yelled in Greek.

"Cara, it's me." A big figure appeared out of the shadows and she stifled a scream. "It's Yannis."

"Oh. Yannis."

"Sorry I startled you. You have a good Greek accent, though. Did you learn that brush-off from a phrase book?"

"Something like that." She blew out a long breath.

"Why are you wandering around out here anyway? I walked you home so you'd be safe at night."

"I'm not under house arrest, you know."

He raised his hands in mock self-defense. "Fine, do what you want. Wander around the island on a Friday night full of drunken tourists who will only see your beautiful red hair and tight dress and won't bother to listen to your Greek phrase book protests." He turned back to his Vespa, which was tucked into a corner along the sidewalk.

"Look, you're right." She hated to admit it. "I need to sleep at my friend's house tonight. *My* place is, um, occupied."

"Occupied? But your blond friend is with Niko." He trailed off into a big grin.

"Yes, yes, Emma and Niko are *together* at my place." She hoped the dim light hid the heat creeping up her cheeks.

"They must have practically run back to beat us there." He shook his head. "Not very considerate. And don't you have separate bedrooms anyway?"

"They weren't *in* her room." Geez, did she have to spell it out for him? "They were apparently overcome with passion and made it as far as the rug in front of the couch. The only thing I saw before I quietly backed away was your buddy's hairy ass!"

Yannis doubled over laughing and stayed that way for a couple minutes. "You poor girl. I'm not surprised. Niko needs to shave three times a day to keep from looking like a gorilla."

"Maybe he should shave his ass," she replied sourly.

That really sent Yannis over the edge. "Oh, Cara, I won't be able to look Niko in the face without laughing."

"What about me? I may have to pull an Oedipus and put my eyes out at the horror." She shook her head. "I hope I can sleep tonight."

"Where *are* you sleeping tonight? You have a friend on the island?" He sounded puzzled.

Cara knew she needed to be more forthcoming, especially if she wanted him to walk her to Athena's house. "I know Athena Kefalas from when I crewed charter boats on Corfu."

"Athena? She's my mother's second cousin. I know where she lives. Do you want a ride to her place?"

"Sure, that would be great." If she could get on the Vespa in her dress.

"Come on." He rolled the scooter onto the street and straddled the seat. She hesitated and then hitched her skirt up, hopping on. She grabbed the edge of the seat for balance.

He cast an amused look back at her. "Are you going to ride with me or run along behind?"

"Ha-ha." She scooted closer to him, the insides of her bare knees gripping his thighs. How long had it been since she'd gripped a man's thighs with hers? Before things had started going south in her marriage, which would be about five years ago. And her husband's thighs had never felt like this, hot and hard with muscle.

"And you have to put your arms around me so we don't tip going around corners."

She hesitated for a second. Of course Greek men didn't put their arms around each other when sharing a scooter, but she wasn't sure she had enough upper-body muscle anymore to hold on to the seat, and she already knew Yannis was a fast driver.

"Niko and your friend are probably finished if you'd rather go back."

"Oh, yuck!" Cara slapped her arms around his waist and felt his laughter. She pinched his very tight abs and he jumped. "That's for bringing up your hairy friend again."

"You sure you're not Greek? You have a well-developed sense of revenge."

"I wish," she muttered.

Yannis started the scooter with a roar and U-turned onto the narrow road. "Hold on, Cara," he called.

She did, and with pleasure. The night wind rushed by them, the smell of the ocean combining with the earthy night-blooming flowers. All they needed was fire to complete the four classical Greek elements.

He turned onto the old stone coastline road overlooking the beach. Out from the shadow of the overhanging houses, Cara tipped her head up to the sky.

There was the fire, the stars that had looked down on Aphrodisias since time began, the stars that had been named and turned into legend by Yannis's ancestors, but never tamed.

Untamed like Yannis. Under his urbane clothes, he was earth with a core of fire, his body radiating heat out to her hands through his silky shirt.

Silk or synthetic blend? She stifled a slightly hysterical giggle at her mind's attempt to bring her body back under control.

But it was a futile attempt, considering how his very presence was softening her like the afternoon sun on the beach. She brushed her hand over his stomach and moved closer, her legs gliding along him.

The scooter jerked slightly, as if he'd tightened his grip on the handlebars.

And he smelled so good, like Greek bay leaves with a hint of lemon. She inhaled again, hungrily but quietly. The machine's vibrations were softening her, too, sending jolts between her thighs as they bounced along the uneven pavement. Her nipples hardened against his back, their sensitive tips aching for his touch.

Soon they would leave the coastline and move inland to Athena's house and her time with Yannis would be over. She'd made it plenty clear to him earlier in the evening that she was just tolerating him for Emma's sake, but the truth was, Cara couldn't handle a man like him.

Coward. Where was the eighteen-year-old girl who'd left home after a lifetime of her parents' squabbles? Where was the twenty-one-year-old woman who had crewed one hundred thousand nautical miles over two oceans and five seas?

Lost. As lost as Odysseus wandering the Aegean for ten years. And it had been exactly ten years since she graduated high school and left home. Funny, she had seen herself more like Odysseus's long-suffering wife, Penelope, weaving, wringing her hands and waiting for her husband to stop lolling around with seductive nymphs and haul his butt back home.

Constantine Constantinos, her very own Greek husband, had never come home from the nymphs, and Cara had done her share of hand-wringing and waiting, choosing to leave the weaving to Athena.

Maybe it was time to take a page out of Homer and indulge in her own lolling. Yannis Petrides was as endlessly seductive as anything from Greek legend.

6

"YANNIS?"

He jolted the scooter again as her breath tickled the back of his neck. She was lucky she hadn't sent him swerving off the road every time she pressed her breasts against him or brushed her cool hands over his belly, mere inches above where he really wanted her to touch him. He'd never had an erection riding along on his scooter before and it wasn't a comfortable sensation.

"What is it?"

"Why don't we stop along at the beach for a minute? I haven't seen the ocean at night, and there's a full moon."

"Are you sure? It's getting late." Yannis desperately thought of things to calm down his arousal. Disgusting things, like slimy piles of seaweed, washed-up octopi, red-headed half-naked mermaids...no, not that last one.

"Yannis, take me to the beach."

He didn't hear much past her first three words. *Yannis, take me.* But he pulled off into one of the parking lots that dotted the shore and cut the engine. "Well, we're here," he said cheerfully, as if he weren't trying desperately not to embarrass himself.

Cara put her hands on his hips and boosted herself off the scooter, surveying the black expanse of water dotted with moonlight. Figured, it was a clear night, perfect for romance.

Yannis guessed he had himself back under control and stood. Then Cara bent over to remove her sexy black sandals, and his control went under. The perfect halves of her bottom outlined in her tight skirt, the slit in the middle hiking up to where he could see what seemed like a meter of pale thigh.

"Oh!" She lost her balance and started to tip forward onto the pavement. He moved quickly and hooked an arm around her waist, dragging her bottom flush up against his crotch again. His erection went from zero to sixty at her closeness.

She gave a little gasp and looked over her shoulder at him, her full lips slightly parted.

"You okay?" It was the only thing he could think of to say. He gently eased her away from him and she nodded. He shoved his hands in his pockets and fervently wished that flat-front, tight-cut pants were not the fashion.

Cara slung her shoes in the small basket behind the seat. "Want to walk?" She was already stepping onto the rocky path leading down to the water, making little exclamations of pain until she rapidly passed onto the sand. "Ooh, the sand's cool."

Maybe he should pack some into his pants. He took a deep breath.

"Yannis, take your shoes off, too."

He conceded and set his Italian leather slip-ons and thin socks next to the back tire. His feet were tougher than hers and the rocks didn't bother him. "Where to?"

She was already pattering away. "The water." She stopped at the water's edge and fearlessly waded in up to her knees. When a larger wave started to crest, she pulled up her skirt even farther. She saw him waiting in the sand. "Come in with me, Yannis. It's lovely and warm."

Not as lovely as she was, her skin silvered by the moon-light. "I can't. I'm not wearing a short dress like you."

She giggled. "And for that, I'm glad."

He couldn't help laughing, as well. This side of Cara was one he'd never seen, happy and playful. "Yeah, lucky for you."

"If you don't want to get seawater on your pants, you could just take them off," she suggested teasingly.

"Oh, yeah? And, what, wander around on the beach in my underwear?" Not that his swimsuit wasn't about the same coverage as his briefs, but psychologically it was very different.

"I will if you will."

Her suggestion zapped him like Cupid's arrow. Her gaze met his, slightly nervous but steady. "And where are we supposed to leave our clothing while we play in the water?"

"Up there." She pointed behind to a spot along the boulders framing the beach. "A cabana—looks like it's empty." She hiked up to the building and once again, he followed.

The empty cabana was a small wooden shack set back among the boulders, providing some privacy for its occupants. The doors were padlocked shut, but he noticed a narrow patio, some beach chairs and a chaise longue. "Are you sure?" He was asking her more than just about a moonlight swim.

"Positive. And I'll go first to prove it." She unfastened the bow behind her neck. The green fabric dropped to her waist, baring her breasts.

Yannis gaped at her. She had a belly button ring—a big round stone that glittered like the waves under the moon. "You have a ring there. I never expected you to have *that*."

She grinned at him. "Why? You thought I was too stuffy to get my navel pierced?"

"Maybe."

"I was a wild girl in my youth."

He laughed. She talked as if she were ancient, instead of a ripe, sexy woman in her prime. "Wild enough to swim naked?"

"Sometimes."

"Still wild enough to swim naked with me?"

"What do you think?" She crossed her forearms under her breasts, offering them up to him.

As he stared, her nipples tightened even further, and he didn't think it was from the cool breeze. "I think yes." As if of its own accord, his hand lifted and hovered above her right breast.

She caught his wrist and pulled his hand to her. They gasped simultaneously. Her breast filled his palm, full and heavy like an apple ripe for the picking. He instinctively thumbed her nipple, making her shudder.

Encouraged, he cupped her other breast, teasing and plucking at the hard berries of her nipples. She tipped back her head. "Oh, Yannis."

He'd never felt skin so soft, so smooth before and closed his eyes in sheer sensual pleasure. Then suddenly, his hands were empty.

Cara had stepped back from him and dropped the rest of her dress to the sand. She spun on her heel and ran toward the water wearing only a tiny pair of black panties. "Last one in is a rotten egg!" she cheerfully called over her shoulder.

She'd literally pulled heaven from his grasp and now she called him a rotten egg? Yannis stripped down to his briefs and charged after her. No matter. A true man of Aphrodisias could pleasure a woman just as easily in the water.

CARA HOPED the crash of the waves masked the beating of her heart. She'd been so, so close to dragging Yannis down on the beach furniture and having her way with him, but panic had made her pull away.

Her feet splashed in the warm surf and she dived into the breaking waves as soon as she was deep enough. So much for her hair. She had bigger concerns. Where was Yannis? She scanned the water. Had she lured him to his doom? What if he'd gotten a cramp from diving in? Or gotten stung by a jellyfish? Sure, they were rare, but you never could tell what the ocean current would bring.

"Yannis?" she called out, stifling a squawk as his head broke the water next to her.

"Miss me?" His hair was black and glossy against his scalp, droplets of water beading on his full upper lip.

"Were you gone?" she retorted automatically.

He gave her what could only be described as a smirk. "You've been waiting for me." He pulled her to him, his hot skin sliding over hers, her nipples catching on the mat of black hair furring his chest.

She swallowed hard. She hadn't realized it until now, but she *had* been waiting for someone to break through her shell of indifference and bring her back to life. Snow White in her glass coffin, Sleeping Beauty in her tower of thorns, and most fitting considering the surroundings, the statue of Galatea brought to life by Aphrodite herself for sake of a love-struck Pygmalion.

No more waiting for someone to rescue her. That *someone* was *her*. Cara Lillian Sokol Constantinos would break through her own self-imposed prison and come back to life.

She laughed giddily, the rusty sound echoing over the water.

"What?" Yannis tightened his grip on her as if afraid she'd run from him again.

"This." She twined her legs around his and grabbed his ears to pull her mouth to his. He eagerly met her kiss, their wet lips softening and sliding on each other, nipping and teasing gently and then more frantically. She wrapped her arms around his broad shoulders, enjoying how easily he supported them both in the water. He still wore his bikini briefs but they couldn't hide the erection pressing on her thigh.

His tongue dived inside her mouth, exploring every corner of that moist cavern and stroking along her own tongue. He tasted of that potent red wine, but of something more, too, something uniquely his own flavor.

She dipped her tongue into his mouth, but he closed his teeth to her when she would continue. She pulled back. "What? Greek men are too macho to get a woman's tongue in their mouth?"

"Believe me, I can't speak for other Greek men, but I'm, uh, pretty ticklish." He gave her a sheepish glance.

"Ticklish? All over?" She stroked down along the hard curve of his back and grabbed two handfuls of firm ass through his briefs. "Here?"

He groaned and thrust his hips into hers. "No, not there."

She slipped her hands under his waistband and touched his bare buttocks, cupping and pinching him. "How about now?"

"*Oxi.*" He shook his head. She smiled as he unknowingly slipped into Greek.

"And here?" She slid her fingers around to the bulge in front, clasping his thick erection and heavy sac.

He was past words now, English or Greek, only gasping as she fondled him. Like most European men, Yannis was uncircumcised, his foreskin and tip obviously extremely sensitive. She played with him, stroking his silky hot skin as his balls tightened under her touch. Slippery fluid leaked from him, mixing with the gentle seawater.

"Stop," he gritted out, clasping her wrist painfully. "Stop now." He was almost panting with the effort to rein himself in.

She let go, not wanting to accidentally hurt him. "Didn't you like that?"

"Too much." He wasn't joking, his face tight and almost pained. "Damned if I'll lose control without pleasing you first."

He reached under the water and actually tore her bikini panties off her, breaking the strings over her hips. The savage act made her gasp. He tossed the black silk away in the water where it quickly sank.

She floated totally naked, the water rushing over the heated skin between her thighs.

"Now." He dragged her to him again. "Wrap your legs around me, and when I make you come the first time, don't scream too loudly. Sound carries over water, and unless you want an audience…?" He lifted a brow, and Cara realized he didn't care if the whole island watched them. She'd let the tiger out of the cage, and it wasn't interested in returning anytime soon. She shook her head. No audience for her.

She wrapped her legs around his waist as he commanded, her pussy resting against his belly, his erection still rock-hard on her bottom.

His fingers dived and unerringly found her clit. She tossed back her head and moaned.

"There. So hot, so wet." He stroked her swollen button leisurely. "Tell me, Cara, *mou,* when I put my mouth here later, will you prove to be a natural redhead?"

She smacked his shoulder, and he laughed. "No matter, you have a redhead's temper. Are you a woman who will scratch my back or bite me when I am pumping between your thighs?"

"Who says you'll find out?" she said with as much bravado as she could muster with his hand pinching her aching clit.

"I do." His fingers sped up. "I knew as soon as you showed me your beautiful tits in the moonlight. You'll let me do whatever I want to you, and then beg me for more."

Cara's protest broke off into a squeal as Yannis bent and captured a nipple in his mouth. His clever mouth teased and sucked her breast into an aching peak as his fingers moved over her clit. She rocked frantically on his belly, his cock rubbing her sensitive inner folds.

Yannis let go of her nipple and she choked back a sob. "That's not enough, is it, baby?" She shook her head, and he worked his hand between their bodies. "Move back for a second."

She eased away and was amply rewarded by a callused finger slipping in and out of her. "More, more," she begged.

"This?" He added another finger and did a little scissoring motion deep inside her that stretched her wide, wider than she'd been for a long time. But still not as wide as his cock would stretch her. She felt his fingers play in her juices, stroking the walls of her passage.

His thumb brushed her clit over and over and he dipped his glossy head to her breasts, caressing his smooth-shaven cheek over each mound. "So soft, so pretty," he murmured, his Greek accent becoming thicker. His cock, still imprisoned in his briefs, bobbed between her buttocks. She wished she could just free him and take him into her body, but obviously had no handy condoms stashed anywhere.

Yannis found a sensitive spot with his fingertips and pressed. Cara yelped. Was that her G-spot? She'd thought that was as mythological as the Minotaur.

Obviously encouraged by her response, he worked it until she was panting and writhing, her hips creating their own tide as they rode up and down his hand.

He captured a nipple in his mouth and sucked hard, his blue gaze silvery in the moonlight. She slipped her fingers through his hair and held him there, his lips and tongue sending currents of lust down to where his fingers pleasured her.

She knew she couldn't last much longer; it had been so long since she'd felt even close to this level of desire. "Yannis!" She was startled to hear the neediness in her voice echo over the water, but was powerless to resist him.

He abandoned her breast and captured her mouth just as her orgasm washed over her with the force of a tidal wave, sweeping her away until she thought she might drown from its power. She screamed his name into the wet cavern of his mouth, begging him to let her go, to make the sensual torment cease.

He was merciless, though, trapping her with a net woven of her own pleasure, making her ride the climactic wave once or maybe even twice more before he stopped.

She released his shoulders and floated in the water, boneless as a jellyfish. Still holding her lower body firmly against him, Yannis withdrew his fingers from her. Instead of washing them off in the ocean, however, he lifted them to his lips and tasted them. "Delicious. Salty and sexy, like the sea."

Cara could only stare at his obvious enjoyment of her. He took her silence for acquiescence and tugged her toward shore.

She finally found her voice. "I guess it's your turn now."

"Who said you don't get another?" He found his footing on the hard-packed sand and swung her naked into his arms, her panties probably washed up on Crete by now. She looped her arms around his neck and looked around anxiously to make sure they were still the only beachgoers.

"Yannis, put me down. I'm too heavy for you." She didn't want to get sand in her more delicate parts when he dropped her.

"You think I am so weak?" He carried her easily uphill on the soft sand toward the cabana.

A rush of excitement ran through her despite her protests as she saw how dark and powerful his hands were on her pale skin. The breeze tightened her nipples, and he slid his hand around to cup her breast again, brushing its sensitive tip. His other hand squeezed her thigh, promising additional delights.

She loosened her grip and combed her fingers through the black mat on his chest, toying with his golden chain and medal before exploring further. His pecs were like rock, capped with tight little peaks that hardened under her leisurely touch.

He groaned deep in his throat. "Cara, you redheaded witch." They had reached the cabana and he set her not-so-steadily on her feet.

She laughed with delight and ran her hands down his abs to his poor, overworked briefs. Despite his halfhearted protests, she stripped them down to his ankles, returning to kneel in front of him. Freed from constriction, he was even thicker and longer than she'd realized, his dark shaft jutting out proudly from a nest of thick black curls that cradled a heavy sac. The head was eggplant-purple and beads of his desire shone in the moonlight.

Yannis was a man on the brink, and Cara was going to push him over it.

"Cara, wait." He stopped her just as she was about to take him in her mouth. "I have something in my wallet. Let me come inside you."

Cara hesitated. To fully let him inside her body? She'd not done that with anyone since Con, and those occasions with him had been memorable only in their mediocrity.

Yannis stood silently, not coaxing or pressuring her, but definitely tempting her. If he was so skilled with his fingers, how much pleasure could he bring her moving inside her, thrusting, pushing, teasing… She stood so abruptly her head spun.

"Yes." That was the only word she spoke, but it unleashed a hurricane. With one smooth move, Yannis set her on the reclining chaise, grabbed his wallet and pulled out a packet.

He set it at the foot of the chaise and lay on his side next to her. "Yes." He echoed her and then dipped his head to hers. Like the Greek pirate he resembled, he plundered her mouth, nipping and sucking her lips until they were sensitive and puffy.

She squirmed under him as he dragged his fingers up her thigh and found her red curls. Without the seawater to wash her juices away, she could feel her moisture slick up his fingertips again as he played with her folds, teasing them apart before landing on her clit. She arched off the chaise. "Oh, Yannis, *now.*"

His laughter was quick and joyful as he protected himself and moved between her thighs. "Now."

She let out a scream as he sank into her with one stroke. Her legs quivered as she hooked them around his waist, not wanting to ever release him. He closed his magnificent eyes and gasped out her name. "Cara, I could *live* inside you."

She closed her own eyes at his heartfelt compliment. Then he began to move, and that was the biggest compliment of all. He was too far gone to hold back and tease her as he had in the water, slamming in and out instead. It was wild and savage with the moon silvering his curls and the waves crashing on the beach in time to her heart.

Cara dug her heels into his ass, her fingernails sinking into his shoulders. His gold medal swayed with his efforts, brushing her face as he moved above her. His cock dipped and plunged, stretching her wider than she'd ever been. Surely, she couldn't come again, not with just his thrusting.

But to her surprise, desire washed over her again. He angled up so the base of his cock bumped her clit. He throbbed and pulsed inside her, grunting as he moved in and out.

Cara slipped her finger between them, desperate to enhance his touch. Her fingernail scraped his cock, and he groaned again. A few quick strokes over her clit and she was as wound as he was.

The knot of tension tightened unbearably and then Cara flew apart underneath him, writhing and twisting as her world narrowed to his body on top of hers and his shaft inside her.

His face pulled into a grimace and he let himself go with a bellow, slamming her deep into the cushion. Cara muffled her scream in his shoulder, clutching and grabbing at him like a wild animal.

He collapsed onto her, his breath hot and fast on her neck. His medal dug into her skin, but it was just proof of his passion for her.

After a few minutes, he stirred and shifted out of her onto his side. His expression was languid and sleepy but sharpened as he looked down at her. "My medal marked your fair skin." He traced a small circle on her chest. "I should have been more gentle, but…" He shook his head. "I didn't mean to be so rough."

Cara's eyes widened as she saw several purple marks on Yannis's chest. "Me, either." She gingerly touched one and he looked down in surprise.

"Cara, you bit me." He noticed the other bruises. "Several times."

Her face heated, and she was glad for the shadows. "Sorry."

He laughed heartily and then winced. "Oh, my back." He sat up and rotated his shoulders to face her. "Tell me, did you scratch me, too?"

She gulped. Yannis looked as if he'd been in a fight with a cougar—and lost. "There are some red lines, yes." Her face had to be as red as his scratches. "They should fade by Monday, and if not…" She gave a casual shrug. "Something for you and the guys at work to joke about when you take off your shirt." She laughed brightly.

He didn't laugh in return. "The guys at work, as you call them, won't be laughing over this because it's none of their damn business. I'll leave my shirt on until they heal. How does the phrase go? I don't kiss and tell. Or tell about anything else."

"Oh," Cara whispered. She seemed to have stumbled on a genuine gentleman. She smiled up at him but broke into a yawn.

"Rest here for a second. I'll get cleaned up and then take you to Athena's house." He pulled a beach blanket over her and went around the corner. The tension that had bugged her since coming to Aphrodisias was finally gone, thanks to her amazing encounter with Yannis. She yawned and closed her eyes to rest for a minute until Yannis came back. Maybe there was something to this whole goddess of love thing....

"HEY, YOU BUMS, get out of here!"

Yannis bolted upright from the chaise, where a very naked Cara curled around him. Her blue eyes opened wide and she dived back under the beach blanket with a squeak.

"Yannis? What are *you* doing here?" His cousin Vasilios regarded him openmouthed. Yannis grabbed for his pants and bit back a curse. He hadn't planned on sleeping in the cabana, but when he'd come back for Cara she'd looked so peaceful he joined her rather than waking her and driving her to Athena's place.

"Vasos, sorry, is this part of your hotel? I didn't know." Yannis hastily buckled his belt and moved in front of the lump under the blankets that was Cara.

"It's okay." Vasos was too distracted now to chew him out, craning his neck to see first off, who the girl under the blanket was and secondly, if she was naked.

"Come with me, Vasos." Yannis caught his cousin by the elbow and steered him around the corner out of sight of Cara, hoping she would take the hint and dress.

"Yanni, who is that?" Vasos asked.

"Nobody you know." Vasos pouted. "Oh, okay, a tourist girl I met." If he didn't give Vasos some information, his cousin's speculations would be worse.

"Figures. You get all the luck."

"Don't give me that bullshit, Vasos, you've gotten more than your share of invitations up to rooms once your shift is finished."

His cousin preened. "Yeah, did I ever tell you about that Spanish girl who was all over me in April?"

"No." Then Yannis had to listen to his cousin's exploits while Cara was hopefully dressing. His cousin had just launched into the part where the girl had danced the flamenco naked for him when Yannis elbowed him.

Cara had found a scarf to cover her wild red hair and large sunglasses to hide her eyes. A lady of mystery, she was wearing the backless gown without a stitch under it, Yannis knew, and in the bright morning sunlight she looked naughty and sexy, a bad girl who'd stayed out all night having sex on the beach.

Vasos gave a low whistle and Yannis elbowed him harder this time. His cousin rubbed the sore spot but cheerfully asked, "Aren't you going to introduce me to your friend, Yannis?"

"No. And keep quiet about this, or else your mother will find out about the naked Spanish dancing girl."

"No fair." Vasos frowned while Yannis offered Cara his arm to help her up the path to where his scooter was luckily still parked.

Yannis turned back to his cousin. *"Efkhareestó, ksathelfos."*

Vasos smiled. "Yeah, you're welcome, cousin. But next time, find a room." He turned away and started dragging the beach furniture out onto the sand.

Cara still hadn't said a word since they woke. "Are you all right, Cara? I'm so sorry I fell asleep. I didn't plan to keep you out all night."

"It's okay." Her voice was morning-rough and sexy. Maybe from screaming his name several times? "I hope Emma's not too worried."

Niko had probably kept Emma too busy to worry, but

Yannis just nodded. Uncle Gus and Aunt Eleni wouldn't say anything to him. After all, he was a grown man and given way more leeway than Uncle Gus's daughters, who would have been locked in their rooms if they'd stayed out all night with a man. Which was probably why they were in Athens and not on Aphrodisias.

Cara made a sound of distress and stopped walking.

"What is it?"

She lifted her foot and wiggled it. "Just a sharp rock."

"Let me check if it broke the skin." He dropped to his knees before her and rested her foot on his knee. He brushed away the sand and checked her skin, but it appeared okay aside from a small red mark. "You might have a little bruise, but no bleeding."

"Thank you, Yannis." She unconsciously flexed her toes on his thigh, making him want to suck on their shiny red tips. He cupped her ankle and stroked her calf up to the hollow behind her knee. Her breath caught, her full lips slightly parted. They were bare and pink and just as sexy as when she'd worn the glossy red lipstick last night. If he ran his hand up just a bit farther, he'd caress her bare bottom.

"Yannis." Her urgent voice snapped him out of where he'd actually begun to stroke the back of her thigh. "Stand up, or else your cousin is going to think you're proposing to me."

He stood so fast, she almost lost her balance. He steadied her and then swung her into his arms with a muttered Greek curse. He carried her up the rocky path and set her next to the scooter. She brushed off her feet and slipped them into the sandals. He slipped on his own shoes, not bothering with his socks.

He hopped on the seat. "Ready?" She settled behind

him and wrapped her arms around his waist. His arousal came roaring back, but too late to do anything about it. He gunned the engine and zoomed away, teeth gritted at the press of her practically naked breasts. Unfair. He was back to where he was yesterday, and his sexy night with Cara had just whetted his appetite for more.

7

"MORE COFFEE, CARA? Cara? Do you want more coffee?" Athena tapped her spoon against the copper coffeepot and Cara jumped.

"What?" She jerked up from where she'd been doodling patterns with her fork in the leftover almond cake crumbs and saw Athena pointing at the long-handled coffeepot. "Oh, no, thank you." She'd been mentally reliving her time on the beach with Yannis and just reached the part where he easily carried her up the sandy slope to the cabana. She checked herself quickly. Athena would doubtless notice her woolgathering.

Athena just smiled at her. "It was good of you to spend the morning with me while Demetria is out. She doesn't like to leave me alone, but she always runs errands on Monday."

"I don't mind visiting at all, and you're looking much better. Not so pale."

Athena clattered the dishes in the sink. "You think so?"

"Oh, yes. When Emma and I first came over, you were white, almost like a ghost."

"Mmm."

Cara stood and carried her plate and cup to the sink. "What would you like to do this morning? We can go for lunch at the café around the corner if you want to get out of the house."

"Yes, that would be nice." Athena washed the dishes in a twinkling of an eye, brushing aside Cara's attempts to help. She was just drying her hands when the old black phone in the front hallway rang.

Cara let Athena answer it while she wiped down the already-gleaming stove and countertop. Her friend's voice rose in bursts of frustration interspersed with silence. Whoever had called was obviously irritating Athena.

"And that is all you have to say to me? I may be an old woman but I am not senile!" The phone slammed in the cradle and Cara rinsed the dishcloth and hung it to dry. Athena stomped back into the kitchen, her black eyes snapping.

"Are you okay, Athena?"

"No, I am not. Some thief is trying to wreck my museum project. We are going out." Athena gripped Cara's elbow with surprising strength and steered her toward the front door.

"Wait, don't you need your walker?"

Athena never broke stride. "That thing makes me look old and weak. You will be my support today."

Cara settled Athena into the front seat of Demetria's blue compact car and started the engine. "Where to?"

"Left here and then the road leading out of town. We are going to visit one of the hill bandits."

"Hill bandits? Didn't they all give up, oh, about a hundred years ago?"

Athena gave her a baleful glance. "Their descendants merely found similar occupations, occupations where they can steal and rob without fear of arrest. When you come to the corner, turn right."

Cara steered along a narrow road through groves of olive trees, their pale green leaves silvered with dust. The road opened to a clearing where construction workers busily put the finishing touches on an ostentatious villa. "Is this where the hill bandit lives?"

"The hill bandit built this overdone heap. And sold it to a bunch of *xenoi*. Park here next to the trailer."

Cara pulled over and stopped, circling around to help Athena out of the low seat. Once standing, Athena moved with surprising agility around the construction supplies and over the uneven ground. She established herself square in the middle of the front veranda, cupped her hands in front of her mouth and shouted in Greek, "Gus Galanopoulos, you old thief, come out and face me like a man!"

Geez, Athena was a master of insults—combining blows to this guy's age, honesty, as well as his manhood in one sentence.

The leaded glass front door slammed open and a man with graying curls strode out wearing a paint-stained, white T-shirt and a tool belt riding low under his straining belly. He tossed his cigarette butt to the ground. "Athena Kefalas, no one comes to my job site and calls me names. Get out of here before you fall and break your other hip."

Cara frowned at him, then remembered that, per Athena's instructions, she wasn't supposed to understand Greek. Still, she could always say she disapproved of this Gus guy's tone.

"You! You must have fallen and broken your head if you think I'll let you get away with stealing that land for my museum."

Oh. Cara nodded to herself. Gus was probably trying to get the museum property for one of his villas he sold to *xenoi,* or foreigners. But Cara had thought the land, at least, was a done deal.

Gus and Athena exchanged a few more insults before Gus bellowed, "Yannis! Yannis! Get down here!"

Yannis? No, the odds were it was a different guy. Half the men on the island were named some version of Ioannis, or John, the other half Nick.

"What, Uncle Gus?" a voice shouted back. It *was* the same Yannis. With odds like that, she should have played the lottery. He came around the side of the house, his sweaty muscular chest outlined in his tight, white T-shirt, his leather tool belt framing his zipper as if to emphasize the mighty nice tool inside. Oh, boy. Cara wanted to strip him naked, except for his belt and work boots, and have her way with him on a stack of drywall.

He spotted her, too, coming to her side. "Cara? What are you doing here?" He had to raise his voice to be heard over the shouting. Although to be honest, Greeks usually talked like that anyway.

"Athena asked me to drive her here. Sorry, I didn't know she'd come to brawl with Gus here. Is he your boss?"

"Yeah, my boss and my uncle."

Gus stopped yelling long enough to tug Yannis away from Cara to stand next to him. As though it was boys against girls. "Yannis, do you see what happens when old crones interfere in men's work?"

Athena narrowed her eyes. "Men's work, hah! A real man would not dishonor the wishes of the dead. *Kyria* Nomikou meant to sell me that land for a museum to honor our ancestors."

"Well, now she's *with* her ancestors, and her grandson wants to sell the land to *me*."

"Such disrespect!" Athena advanced on Gus, her gnarled forefinger pointing menacingly at his nose. In her long, black dress and with her wild, dark eyes, she looked like a witch about to curse him. "You bring shame to our island."

Gus involuntarily took a step back, his hands twitching

in the sign to repel the Evil Eye that a lot of Greeks believed in. And Athena was looking mighty evil at this point.

Cara shot Yannis a glance. He seemed more amused than frightened, but then he probably didn't know Athena as well as she did.

"*Kyria* Kefalas." Gus held up his hands in reconciliation. "There is no shame in building houses and making jobs for our young people here on Aphrodisias. If all our children leave to find work, our island will slowly wither away."

"My museum will give them jobs, too, and not ones that dry up once the houses are finished. And who can afford these homes anyway?" She gestured at the immense villa with contempt. "Foreigners, who were happy to invade us and starve us when you and I were young. *Xenoi,* who come for the summer and leave them empty for the rest of the year. Empty houses on an empty island. Is that what you want?"

"Where is your grandson Spiro? Where are my daughters? They are all in Athens. Will they ever move back home?" Gus threw up his arms. "Who knows? But right now there is nothing here for my daughters unless they want to be shop clerks or hotel maids. And they do not. Does Spiro want to be a bartender or a tour boat captain?"

Athena shook her head. "No, but Gus, this is not the way—"

"Eh! Do not talk to me of empty islands, then. I *will* buy that land, and I *will* build those villas. And if I have to sell them to the man in the moon, I will." He turned on his heel and left.

Athena pursed her lips and headed back to the car. Cara started to follow her to make sure she wouldn't trip, but Yannis caught Cara's elbow, stroking the tender skin in the crook of her arm. "Cara."

"Yannis." Her whisper came out huskier than she planned.

"God, you smell great." He tipped his head down and inhaled deeply. "What is that, peaches?"

"Yeah, but you smell great, too."

He laughed. "Oh, yeah, construction work in the summer makes me smell like a flower."

He did smell wonderful, like sun and warm leather, sweat and sexy man. "Cara, I think my uncle and Athena are fighting over some property, but I don't want it to interfere with us."

"Me, either." She couldn't stop staring at his lips.

"I had a great time Friday night, and I want to see you again." Both of them were breathing faster, and she knew exactly how he wanted to see her. Naked and underneath him.

"What time do you finish today?"

"Three, but I might have to come back in the evening, depending on what the crew gets done."

"I'll meet you here at three, then we can go for a drive in the country." She was getting him naked as soon as possible.

"But Cara, I really should go home and shower first, and then we can…" His protest died as she ran her tongue around her lips suggestively. "Three o'clock."

"Don't be late." She swung her hips as she walked away. He was silent for a second and then started shouting orders to the crew to work faster.

She tamped down her grin as she reached the car, where Athena was waiting for her.

"So, Karoleena, you've met Yannis Petridis before? His mother is my second cousin."

"Yeah, his friend Niko is spending time with Emma." She gave a casual shrug. "We met that way."

Athena sat silently for a couple minutes as they drove back into town. "Karoleena, I have another favor to ask you. Spend time with Yannis. As much as you can."

"What?" Cara stared at her friend for a second and then had to swerve to avoid a stray goat.

"Yannis works for his uncle. He may tell you things about this project we are fighting over. And you can make up things to tell him. We can confuse Gus—not a difficult thing to do," she muttered.

"I don't know…" Cara didn't want to seem eager to help Athena's machinations. Heaven only knew where *that* would lead them.

"Please, *chriso mou,* it would help the weaving and women's art museum. There is nothing here on Aphrodisias to celebrate our mothers' achievements."

"Not my mother. Her only achievement was to make our lives miserable." She bit her lip, but the bitterness had burst from her before she could stifle it. She focused out the windshield and steered toward town.

"Karoleena." Athena's voice was gentle. "Karoleena, from what you have told me, your mother was a very insecure woman, and your father did nothing to help her feel better."

Huh. That was an understatement. From what she could remember and then later piece together, her father had had a string of bimbos on the side for many years.

"And I have always considered you to be a Greek woman."

"Why? Because I was once married to a Greek man?"

"No. You have the soul of a Greek woman. Strong yet caring. Proud yet humble. Fiery yet sweet."

Cara shook her head. "You're giving me too much credit. I'm not any of those."

"Bah!" Athena threw up her hands. She was the only person Cara knew who could get away with saying "bah." Athena continued, "I see it in you. I could see it in you when Constantinos brought you home, and I see it still."

The dusty road blurred into mud as her eyes filled. She hurriedly pulled over to stop. "Oh, Athena, I was so weak. You don't know…" She let out a sob.

Athena pulled her into her arms, tugging Cara's head to rest on her pillowy bosom. "You think I didn't know? I, Athena Kefalas, knew everything."

"Everything?" She couldn't have.

"Everything, darling. Why do you think I made you fattening milk shakes all the time? Why do you think I always told you long, boring stories right after breakfast and lunch? You were such a polite girl to listen to me when all you wanted to do was run to the bathroom and get rid of all my good cooking. I knew it all."

"I had bulimia." It was a relief to admit it.

"Yes." Athena's chin bobbed against her curls. "Ox-hunger—a word I wish we Greeks had never had to invent. I told Constantinos you needed help, that you were desperately unhappy, but—"

"All he could see was that I was thin and pretty and looked good in my party dresses."

"Blind, stupid man, concerned only with himself!" Athena spit out. "His father was my cousin, but that did not make me blind to his faults after being his housekeeper for fifteen years. He did not see your hair I pulled from the drain, your bones sticking through your skin."

She took Cara's shoulders and pushed her away, her black eyes piercing Cara. "Constantinos failed you. *I* failed you." She overrode Cara's protests. "No! It has worn heavy on my heart since you left Greece. Seeing you so healthy and well has lightened my spirits." She yanked Cara close again and kissed her on each cheek, wiping away her tears. "Now if only I could see you happy."

"I am happy," Cara protested.

"No. You are not miserable. That is not the same thing." Athena smiled. "But you *will* be happy. I promise."

CARA FINISHED winding her hair into long ringlets and stood back to survey the results in her bathroom mirror. Her white, sleeveless, linen blouse ended right above the waistband of her pale peach shorts.

Her cheeks were flushed and pink, and she had the same kind of giddy relief that had once come with her eating disorder, but without the accompanying shame.

She had admitted all of it to Athena, and Athena hadn't judged her harshly. In fact, Athena had known it already and had worried over her. Just like a mother. The sly old lady. Cara laughed out loud.

Geez, all of Athena's excruciatingly long stories about her children, grandchildren, cousins, Greek mythology, even the in-depth descriptions of how to string looms for different tapestries had been an attempt to get Cara even a bit of nutrition from her meals.

Athena was a plotter, like her mythological namesake. Was she encouraging Cara to see Yannis for cloak-and-dagger reasons, or was her matchmaking radar picking up some interesting signals?

Cara decided she didn't care and slicked some coppery gloss over her lips. She tied a peach silk scarf over her hair for the drive and grabbed her sunglasses.

When she exited the bathroom, she found Emma in the kitchen pouring some fizzy lemonade into a blue wineglass.

"Hey, Cara, how was your day with Athena?" She began slicing some ripe melon and arranging the pieces on a blue-and-yellow stoneware plate sitting on the countertop.

Cara smiled. How to describe the day's ups and downs? She settled for the simple. "We took a drive, saw Yannis, and I'm going to meet him in a few minutes."

Emma looked sidelong at her and grinned. "And you said you didn't like him. Shows what the romantic air on this island can do for you." She opened a carryout container and set a few slices of baklava and *galaktobouriko* in the middle of the melon slices. The pastries were oozing honey and nuts.

"Fancy," Cara commented. "Do you have a guest coming over?" If it was Niko again, she'd be sure to listen carefully at the door before entering.

"Nope." Emma rinsed off her hands and dried them on a towel. "All for me. I'm just as special as any guest."

Cara stopped. She'd never thought of it that way. Until she'd come to Aphrodisias, food was a necessary evil to be battled for sustenance. But to make it beautiful for herself? She'd never cared enough to try.

"Here." Emma pushed the plate toward her. "A small snack before you go. Who knows when you two will come up for air?" She laughed, and Cara joined in before hesitating over the food.

"Come on," Emma coaxed. "The old lady at the market said it was the freshest melon in Greece, and the bakery clerk said the honey for the pastries was gathered by genuine vestal virgins."

"What? There's no such thing anymore...." Cara stopped when Emma broke into laughter. "Ha-ha."

"Gotcha. Lucky for the bees, there's a shortage of

lifelong virgins around. But that doesn't mean the desserts aren't fabulous," Emma said.

Cara took a deep breath. The presentation was lovely, and at least the fruit was healthy. "Sure." She took a bite of the orange melon, its juices light and sweet in her mouth. "Yum."

Emma took a forkful of the custard pastry. "And a bit of *galaktobouriko*. You said that was your favorite."

"Okay." Cara ate the creamy filling and crunchy phyllo dough topping. It was delicious, but it didn't make her want to eat a whole pan to cover up whatever else was bothering her. "Thanks, Emma. That was great."

"Isn't it?" Emma began eating her snack with enjoyment. "Sometimes, even a taste is enough."

Cara nodded. "There was a time for me when that wasn't the case." Athena knew, why not Emma?

Emma sipped her lemonade. "No?"

"I had a problem with knowing when to stop eating, and then I felt bad, so I'd get rid of the food, um, the wrong way."

"Yeah." Her friend nodded. "I had a roommate in under-grad who did the same thing. It took us a while to figure out what she was up to, but when we did, we dragged her to campus health services. Unfortunately, they have a lot of experience with this. Are you okay now?"

Emma's matter-of-fact response silenced Cara for a minute while she blinked back tears. "Yes, I'm getting there. I haven't purged in a couple years."

"Good." Emma set down her lemonade and hugged her. "So this goes double for you." She gestured to the pretty dishes and artfully arranged food. "Make it nice for your-self. Food isn't your enemy anymore. You deserve to enjoy it. After all, it's giving you the energy to romp around with Adonis."

Cara gave her a mock frown. "Yannis."

"Right, right. You know my Greek is terrible." Emma winked and nibbled at the baklava. "Now go have fun."

FUN WAS CERTAINLY on Cara's mind as she pulled next to where Yannis was parked at his job site. She cut the engine and listened to the Greek birds singing in the trees until they were drowned out by angry bellowing.

A man was giving the crew hell, calling them the laziest SOBs on the island and questioning if they planned to finish sometime before New Year's Day. It sounded like Yannis.

The workers obviously didn't appreciate it, yelling in response. Finally Yannis shouted for them all to go home since they weren't bothering to work anyway.

Cara watched in amusement as the crew members tossed their tools in the pickups and crammed into the cabs. A couple grinned at her and one even whistled as they left. She ignored them, only having eyes for the rumpled, sweaty, sexy man coming toward her.

She climbed out of the car. "Hey, Yannis." She wanted to lean casually on the hood, but knew better in the afternoon heat.

"Cara." He stopped short when he saw her, his face ruddy from either heat or anger, plaster dust frosting his hair. She could guess what he'd look like when he was older, and he'd still be extremely sexy. "You're here."

"I told you I'd be here at three, but I didn't think you'd fire your crew just to get them out of the way."

He laughed, his tension dissipating. "Eh, they'll be back tomorrow. Tonight they'll just sit around complaining about me while they drink beer and watch football matches on satellite. No big deal."

"So they left you here all alone and unprotected?" She

ran her hand over his chest, the thin T-shirt molding to every muscle. "Strange women might come by and take advantage of you."

He groaned and caught her wrist as she found his nipple under the worn cotton. "Cara, I really should go home and clean up. It will only take me a few minutes."

She gestured to the water cooler in the bed of his truck. "Do you have water in there?"

"Yeah, some."

"You can wash the worst of the dirt off with that."

He threw up his hands. "I give up. Where *do* you want to go with me looking like this?"

"Somewhere alone."

His eyes widened. That obviously hadn't been the answer he expected. "Uh…"

"You've lived all your life on this island. Surely you know somewhere private, some place where no one ever goes."

He slowly nodded. "My grandfather's vineyard up in the hills. He's visiting his sister over on Naxos for the week."

"I assume this is your truck. Let's take it. I don't know if Athena's car can make it." Cara decided to confess her friend's schemes. She and Yannis could have at least that much honesty between them. "She was more than happy to loan it to me since she wants me to pump you."

He grinned, and Cara started to blush at the connotation. "For information, I mean. She wants to know what your uncle is up to."

"So I have to choose between being pumped and being loyal to my family?" He shook his head in mock dismay. "No choice any man should have to make."

"Oh, you!" She balled her fist and thunked him in the chest.

He grabbed her hand and kissed her wrist, his hot lips sliding over her tender skin. "You smell wonderful again— this time, like ripe, sweet melon."

"I ate some before I came here." Her hand fluttered open and he nuzzled her fingertips.

"Such pretty hands, so pale and delicate. I can practically see the blood running through your veins." He laced his fingers through hers, his rough palm against hers. "Much too fine to press on mine."

"That's not true. You work for a living, and you should be proud of that. Do you think women want a soft-handed man?" When she had been crewing sailboat charters, her hands had been as tough as his.

"I don't care what other women want. I only care what you want." He slowly drew her closer until mere inches separated their bodies. "What do you want, *latria mou?*"

He had called her his darling. How sweet. She went up on tiptoes and kissed him. It was what their first kiss should have been, tender and sweet, only their lips and hands touching. The birds had started to sing again, and Cara felt almost dizzy with their sound and the fecund smell of the trees and wildflowers.

He made no effort to deepen the kiss, only brushing his mouth over hers despite the desire radiating off him. It was absolutely the most romantic kiss she'd ever had, and she almost cried out in disappointment when he lifted his face from hers.

"Come to the vineyard with me before I lose control and take you here on your car. We'd rather not get painful metal burns in sensitive body parts."

Cara giggled at his welcome humor. Humor, she could handle. Desire, or even blinding lust, she could handle. Tenderness, she wasn't so sure. She let go of his hand and took some blankets from her car. Yannis set them in the pickup bed and helped her into the front seat.

Yannis vaulted into the driver's seat.

"Do you like surprises?"

"The truth?" He gave her another quick smile as he navigated a rough road leading uphill. "Not usually. I know what I want to do and how to do it. But you, I don't know what to expect. In the nightclub Saturday, you looked at me like you hated me, and half an hour later, we're naked in the ocean."

"You surprised me, too." She defended herself. "I thought you would be…" How did she describe a male bimbo without being deathly insulting? "Not quite so generous with your, um, togetherness skills."

He laughed heartily. "Thought I'd be, how do you say, a loser in bed?"

"Well…" She stared out the windshield, willing her blush to subside.

"Cara, I am a builder. I can make wonderful things, but only with good-quality materials. And you, *chriso mou,* are excellent material." He stroked her knee with his free hand, gliding up her thigh. "Your skin is smooth Greek marble, your eyes and hair the finest tints." He slid his hand between her legs. "And here—" he rubbed the center seam of her shorts "—the fountain of inspiration that quenches my thirst."

Cara gripped his wrist as he traced the peach fabric. "Yannis…"

"Uh-uh." He removed his hand and put it back on the steering wheel. "This time, we take our time. And today, we have all the time in the world."

8

"HERE WE ARE." YANNIS parked under a grove of olive trees next to the vineyard and helped Cara down from the truck.

Cara surveyed the neat rows of vines stretched up the rocky hill, the leaves dusty from the typically dry summer weather. It was silent except for birdsong and the occasional buzz of an insect. No one was within miles, as far as she could tell. "What a lovely place, so peaceful."

He smiled over at her from where he unloaded the blankets. "That's because it's not harvest time. Get my grandfather out here bossing his crew and you'd wish yourself anywhere else."

"Sounds as if you've been on his crew a few times."

"More than a few." He knelt and spread the blankets under an ancient olive tree.

Cara rubbed the gnarled trunk and gazed up into the silvery green leaves, its slightly bitter scent reminding her that not everything beautiful could be sweet.

A gentle touch on her shoulder brought her out of her introspection. She turned to see Yannis staring at the tree, as well. "My *pappous*—grandfather, that is—says the tree is almost two thousand years old."

"No, really?" Cara peered at the sturdy trunk. "I didn't know they could grow so old."

Yannis nodded. "One of the university agriculture professors came to the island several summers ago and studied them. This is the oldest of all."

Two thousand years old. Standing silent and still in an olive grove bordering a vineyard, bearing fruit year after year. How many people had rested under its canopy, laughing, weeping, making love? It was beyond Cara's grasp. Sometimes she couldn't bear to contemplate the past several years or consider what the future might bring.

"So quiet, Cara *mou?*"

She quickly pasted a bright look on her face and turned to him. "Just admiring the tree."

"Yes." He clasped her shoulders in his hands and kissed her forehead, somehow knowing her solemn mood. "Something so old, so valuable. It can make thoughtful people melancholy when they contemplate what times the tree has passed through."

"The tree endured more than we'll ever see."

He shrugged. "Maybe, maybe not. The tree cannot laugh, the tree cannot cry, the tree cannot love someone or lose them."

Or lose people they didn't love, but had once upon a time. What was worse? The anguish of lost love or continued guilt? She didn't know.

But Con was gone, and she was here, and with someone else, who seemed very nice, nicer than she deserved. She stopped herself. Emma was right, and so was that counselor she'd seen. She did deserve better.

And Yannis was her "better."

YANNIS WONDERED what else had put the serious look on her face. Surely it had to be more than an old olive tree? But she smiled at him with some effort that gradually lightened. "You must be uncomfortable after a hot day at work. Give me the water, Yannis."

He handed her a jug that had been sitting in the back of the pickup most of the day. "I have bottled water that probably tastes better."

"We're not drinking this, Yannis. I'm going to clean you up. Take off your shirt."

Her wet hands rubbing over him? He almost pulled off an ear taking off his T-shirt. He subtly flexed his chest and arms as her blue eyes grew smoky with desire. "Oh, Yannis." She circled him slowly, her finger brushing through his chest hair and toying with his medal. "You're even more sexy in the sunlight." She traced one of the healing marks on his back. "I'm sorry about your back."

"I'm not. It'll be one of my best memories."

"Good." She stood in front of him again and lifted the jug. "Bend over so I can clean you up."

He did, and she poured the cool water over his back and into his short, sweaty hair. She must have set the jug down since she began massaging the water into his hot skin. He sputtered as some ran into his face, and stood up and wiped it away.

"Oh, dear." She frowned. "The water seems to be running down below your waist. That can't be comfortable." She fumbled at his jeans and he quickly unfastened them. He reached down to undo his leather work boots, but she stopped him. "I, uh, want you to leave your boots and jeans on." Color blossomed in her cheeks. "I thought you looked really sexy at work that way."

"Okay." He couldn't help the smile that spread over his face. So Cara had a construction worker fantasy. "I'd wear my tool belt, but it might get in the way."

"I know." She looked disappointed.

"But I'd be happy to let you work with my tool."

Her red brows drew together in puzzlement. "I've never

built anything before…." Her face cleared as he roared with laughter. She scoffed, "You and your jokes. We'll see who's laughing in a minute."

"Nobody," he countered. "Laughing is not the noise I had in mind." He shoved down his pants and briefs. "Come to me, pretty Cara. Let this hard, sweaty construction worker build something good for you." He reached for her, but she ducked away and he couldn't chase her with his jeans at his ankles.

Cara was staring at his erection. "I just realized this was the first time we've seen each other naked in the daytime. You're beautiful."

His cock bobbed up even higher at her rapt admiration but to his annoyance, he felt a blush creep up his face. "Beautiful is for women. Women like you." He made another grab for her, but she easily evaded him.

"You'll hurt yourself if you fall now. And I don't want anything to happen to your lovely tool."

"I'll put it away and drive you back to your car unless I see you naked in the next sixty seconds." They both knew it was an empty threat, but she started unbuttoning her blouse.

The upper curves of her breasts appeared first, then the full mounds encased in ivory lace. She shrugged the blouse off and dropped it to the blanket.

She turned her back to him and unfastened the bra closure, the bra falling from her shoulders. Her back was great, soft and smooth, but he still couldn't see her breasts.

He craned his head, but then she was unfastening her shorts and her ass came into view. *Gamoto!* She was wearing a matching thong and the ivory lace made her appear naked from the back. Her skin was smooth as the beach and her hair red as the sunset. She gave a wiggle and dropped her shorts to the blanket.

He couldn't stand it anymore. Hiking up his jeans just enough not to trip, he moved behind her. She squealed in surprise as he cupped both breasts with one hand and dragged her against him. His cock pressed into the perfect flesh of her ass, the thong a laughable barrier. Speaking of barriers...he reached into his wallet and pulled out the brand-new condom he'd stashed there after the beach.

He quickly rolled it on while he played with her nipples. Damn, she felt great, warm and round and soft with tips tightening under his fingers, but he still hadn't seen her naked in the daylight.

She then made low moaning noises and rotated her butt back into his erection. Encouraged, he dipped his other hand down the front of her thong and stroked the little button there as he licked and sucked her neck. He told her in very explicit and graphic Greek exactly what he was going to do to her and how much she'd like it, knowing she'd be shocked if she understood him. But something of his message must have gotten across because she clutched his arm and came under his fingers, her juices creamy-wet and hot. He held her steady until she stopped pulsing.

He switched to English to make sure she was ready. "Take me into your pussy now, Cara."

His cock twitched at her sexy groan, her face still flushed from her orgasm. "Yannis, I'm going to fall."

"Grab the tree for balance." She clutched the gnarled trunk of the olive tree and braced herself. He hooked her thong to the side and nudged her thighs apart with his knee. "Open for me."

She immediately tipped her ass up to him. He eased between her folds and sank into her warm, welcoming passage. "Oh, Cara." He wanted to cry, scream, explode at the perfection.

"Yes, Yannis." She held perfectly still for a minute, her flesh pulsing around him. Then she began to rock her hips, his cock slipping out until he couldn't stand it and rammed back inside her.

"Don't tease me, Cara. I need you too badly." His admission shocked him, but he was too far gone to censor himself. He'd been thinking of her since their night on the beach, and he'd been semiaroused since she'd promised to meet him at the job site. And now here he was, taking her against an olive tree like an oversexed, half animal, half man satyr. Legends told that they had uncontrollable, permanent erections, and since meeting Cara, he could sympathize.

"I need you, too." Her knuckles were white against the tree trunk. "Move inside me. Take me hard."

The aroma of the olives and grapes, the light buzzing of the bees, while his dark, swollen erection plunged into Cara's perfect pale body was too much for him. She was his wood nymph, his obsession. He succumbed to the drunken lust pounding through him and slammed in and out of her, his rough hands fondling her delicate breasts as they swayed in time with his thrusts.

He pinched her nipples hard and was rewarded by a fresh gush of her juices to slick his way. He changed his angle to rub deep inside her and she moaned, her pussy beginning to clench around him.

Nuzzling her damp red curls out of the way, he licked her neck, tasting her sweat and inhaling the scent that was only hers. "That's it, baby." He realized he was speaking in Greek, but couldn't help himself. "So pretty, so soft, so hot." He encouraged her with words and actions as she writhed in front of him. "Come for me, sweet Cara. Let my cock give you pleasure."

Quivers built inside her, cupping and squeezing him until his balls tightened and threatened to spill over. He bit her earlobe and clamped his fingers over the swollen peaks of her breasts.

She screamed his name, startling the birds from the trees, and bucked wildly. He grabbed her around the hips and pounded into her, burying himself to the hilt. She was so tight and wet…he fought off his orgasm for a few seconds to give her more pleasure, but then a red wave rose before his eyes and he exploded blindly, bellowing with just as much force as his seed erupting from him.

He couldn't tell where his flesh ended and hers began as they were locked together in a wild, savage climax. Aeons passed, and then they were both trembling. It was almost too hard to stand. He eased from her and quickly disposed of the condom in a trash bag before taking her hands. "Come, lie down."

He helped her sit on the blankets and feasted his eyes. Cara was perfect. Her full breasts were tipped with hard peaks still rosy-pink from his touch. Her belly was firm but curvy, the bright blue jewel winking sexily up at him, leading down to a damp red nest.

She followed his gaze. "Yes, I am a natural redhead," she said drily.

"I wasn't thinking that." He finally unlaced his boots and kicked off the rest of his clothing. He sat next to her and brushed aside a red curl before pressing a kiss to her shoulder.

"No? Then what were you thinking?" She ran her finger down his chest, stopping just below his belly button.

He swallowed hard. "I was thinking you look wonderful, and I want to toss you down on the blanket and start all over again, this time with some finesse."

She slowly lay back on her elbows and stretched her arms over her head, pulling her breasts up high and firm. "Sometimes, finesse is overrated."

He was glad she thought so, since he hadn't shown any so far the two times he'd made love to her. Stretching out next to her, he propped himself on his elbow and looked down at her. "Stay with me this afternoon. I can't get enough of you." It was true. He'd dreamed of her the past few nights and woken up with his dick so hard he could drive nails with it.

He'd never been so obsessed with a woman before and didn't know if she felt the same. He didn't know how long she'd be in Aphrodisias, or even how long she would want him for a lover. Uncertainty was not a familiar or welcome feeling for a man who designed his life with the same care he designed his buildings.

CARA STARED UP at Yannis, who was wearing a frown. "Yannis?" Her finger traced the furrow between his eyebrows. "Something bothering you?"

He shrugged. "Just wondering how much time we have."

"Athena's not expecting her car back for a while. I told her and Emma we were going out for the evening. Why? Do you have to be back for something?"

"No." He flopped onto his back and stared up at the sky. "Men don't answer to anyone but themselves."

"Is that so?" Cara sat up and stroked the hard muscles in his chest, enjoying how the black hair curled around her fingers, his gold medal glittering up at her.

"Yes." His breathing sped up, though, especially when she found his coppery nipples. She knelt next to him and licked one. He groaned and threaded his hands through her hair. She sucked his nipple until it peaked in her mouth and then moved to his other one. Instead of sucking it, she bit it, making him flinch.

"And what do these men do when they have no one to answer to? No one to…relieve…their loneliness?" Cara slid her hand down his belly and cupped his penis. He was already half-hard and quickly filled under her gentle touch. "Do they do this?" She stroked him slowly. "Have you done this, Yannis?"

"What?" His blue eyes were dazed.

She stopped caressing him for a second. "Have you touched yourself when the need becomes too great?"

He nodded slowly, his hips jerking.

"When was the last time you couldn't stand to go another minute without it?"

"Yesterday. And the day before." He swallowed hard as she discovered a silvery bead on his tip and she massaged it into the skin there.

"Yesterday and the day before?" They'd just had sex Saturday night. Her insides quivered. A man who wanted sex every day was a new and delicious creature to savor. "What made you need it so bad?"

"You." His gaze cleared. "I dreamed you were fucking me and woke up about to come. I used my hand and wished it was you."

Wow. "I suppose your hand is better than nothing." She licked a trail down his stomach and stuck her tongue in his belly button. "But not as good as this."

She lifted her mouth and planted it firmly around his cock. He let out a cry of half pleasure, half pain. He was salty and slick, his foreskin slipping back and forth over the taut head as she moved him deeper into her throat.

He burst into frantic Greek, his fingers tightening

GET FREE BOOKS and FREE GIFTS WHEN YOU PLAY THE...

SLOT MACHINE GAME!

Just scratch off the silver box with a coin. Then check below to see the gifts you get!

YES! I have scratched off the silver box. Please send me the 2 free Harlequin® Blaze™ books and 2 free gifts (gifts are worth about $10) for which I qualify. I understand I am under no obligation to purchase any books, as explained on the back of this card.

351 HDL EXEH   **151 HDL EXFU**

FIRST NAME	LAST NAME

ADDRESS

APT.#   CITY

STATE/PROV.   ZIP/POSTAL CODE

7	7	7	**Worth TWO FREE BOOKS plus 2 BONUS Mystery Gifts!**
🍒	🍒	🍒	**Worth TWO FREE BOOKS!**
♣	♣	🍒	**Worth ONE FREE BOOK!**
🔔	🔔	🍒	**TRY AGAIN!**

www.ReaderService.com

(H-B-05/09)

DETACH AND MAIL CARD TODAY!

The Harlequin Reader Service — Here's how it works:

Accepting your 2 free books and 2 free gifts (gifts valued at approximately $10.00) places you under no obligation to buy anything. You may keep the books and gifts and return the shipping statement marked "cancel". If you do not cancel, about a month later we'll send you 6 additional books and bill you just $4.24 each in the U.S. or $4.71 each in Canada. That is a savings of 15% off the cover price. It's quite a bargain! Shipping and handling is just 25¢ per book. You may cancel at any time, but if you choose to continue, every month we'll send you 6 more books, which you may either purchase at the discount price or return to us and cancel your subscription.

*Terms and prices subject to change without notice. Prices do not include applicable taxes. Sales tax applicable in N.Y. Canadian residents will be charged applicable provincial taxes and GST. Offer not valid in Quebec. Credit or debit balances in a customer's account(s) may be offset by any other outstanding balance owed by or to the customer. Please allow 4 to 6 weeks for delivery. Offer available while quantities last.

almost painfully in her hair. "Slow down, slow down."
She did as he asked, wanting to pace herself. Then he
lifted her off him. She let go, not wanting to hurt him.
"Come here." His big hands manhandled her thighs apart
until she knelt facing away from him.

She wasn't sure what he had in mind until he slid under
her and parted her folds. Her squawk of surprise quickly
turned into a moan as he sucked her clit for the first time.
She wavered between embarrassment and lust at the realization she was sitting on his face and he was enjoying it,
as well, judging from his deep purple erection and his
hums of satisfaction.

He gently pushed on her back until she leaned forward
over his body and braced her hands on either side of his hips.
His cock beckoned her as it had before, much bigger than
any other she'd seen. He glistened in the sunlight, thick and
turgid, with heavy distended veins feeding his desire.

Cara dropped her head and panted as Yannis gave
several long licks, spearing his tongue deep inside her.
She couldn't keep away from him for one more second and
sucked his cock into her mouth. His muffled cry encouraged her as she bobbed up and down his shaft.

He was so hot and hard and wet. No wonder she'd been
filled to the bursting point. All of him, inside her on the
beach, against the tree…her thighs quivered as he enthusiastically tongued her clit. She was about to come again—
she couldn't believe it, but there…oh, there it was. Rays
of the sun burst orange against her closed eyes as his heat
rolled up from his tongue and throughout her whole body.
She trembled on top of him, crying out against his cock.
She felt him shake and knew he was going to lose control,
as well. She sucked him hard. His moan vibrated her pussy
and he exploded up into her mouth, flooding her with his

warm, salty essence. He pulsed between her lips for several long seconds and then gave a shuddering sigh.

Somehow, she didn't know how, she climbed off him and collapsed next to him. He stroked her hair. "*Fos ton mation mou,*" he murmured.

"What?" She hadn't heard him.

"Light of my eyes, Cara *mou.*"

"Oh, Yannis." She closed her eyes, and he tugged her so her head rested on his shoulder. She'd never been anyone's light of anything before, but lying in a sunny Greek olive grove with a kind, sexy man, it seemed perfectly right.

9

"THIS IS THE PLACE. The land where I am to build my museum—if those *men* don't interfere with my plans." Athena scowled at the scrubby vista in front of them, her arms folded over the ample bodice of her black dress.

Cara nodded. It looked like the rest of rural Aphrodisias, yellowed grass and gnarled old trees, like the vineyard where she and Yannis had made love only a few days ago. Like the vineyard, no buildings dotted the land, and a mostly dried-up stream drizzled through one side of the property. Hardly turf to go to war over, but Athena and Gus had staked their positions. "Athena, I don't see why I can't just go to *Kyria* Nomikou's heirs and make them a better offer. I have the money to do it, you know that."

"No! Absolutely not." Athena held up her hand in denial. "I would never take your money for my own gain."

"You could pay me back—" Cara was once again silenced by an imperious hand.

"I thank you, but no. I have my own money for this, and I will make it work. You are a young woman and need to pay for your education."

"Athena…" Cara rolled her eyes. She had enough money to pay for the education of every single kid on Aphrodisias plus all of their kids and grandkids. And in a weird twist of fate, her anonymous scholarship fund was currently paying for Yannis's cousins to study in Athens.

But Athena had narrowed her eyes and was staring over the land, her gaze mapping every contour and valley. "*Kyria* Nomikou was the oldest woman on the island and the property had been in her family since anyone could remember—hundreds of years."

"Sure." Until foreigners had become interested in buying property on Aphrodisias, islanders had rarely sold land, keeping it for their sons and grandsons. Foreigners—now Cara was starting to think like an Aphrodisian, regarding outsiders with suspicion.

"But I seem to recall a curious thing—this land was only passed down to the oldest daughter—not to the sons."

Cara raised an eyebrow. That was certainly unusual in the traditionally patriarchal Greek society. "Was that even legal back then?"

Athena shrugged. "We Aphrodisians are the ones who say what is legal on our island. Now if only my dear mother were still alive. She and *Kyria* Nomikou were great friends and that is partly why *Kyria* Nomikou agreed to sell the land to me."

"If she'd kept the property so long, why would she sell it to you?"

"Ah…" Athena tapped her chin. "She had no daughters and no granddaughters—only boys to inherit. She said it was important to keep the property for the honor of women, like it had been in the old days."

Cara frowned. "The old days? How old?"

"Maybe even back to the times of the ancients. The old lady used to brag about how her family was descended from the priestesses of Aphrodite, but half the men on the island used to claim they were descended from Zeus or some such nonsense." The old lady cackled. "I saw enough of their so-called lightning bolts to know *that* was a lie."

Cara covered her eyes. Another appalling image that needed burning from her brain. "Oh, Athena," she whimpered in protest.

"Eh, don't be so missish. We're neither of us virgins anymore, and you should be glad of it, considering how that Yannis Petrides looks at you."

"Really?" Cara peeped out from her fingers. "How does he look at me?"

Athena smirked. "Like you're a platter of pastries and he's been herding goats up in the hills for months."

Cara couldn't help but giggle as her stomach growled. Food, food and more food. Athena had served her some *kourabiethes* with their midmorning coffee.

Athena overheard that noise. "So come on! The sooner you help me think of something, the sooner I can cook you a nice lunch," she wheedled. "And you can get back to your young man."

"He won't be happy if his uncle's plans fall through," Cara warned her.

"Don't worry about your Yannis. You have been truthful with him about helping me build our museum."

"It's practically the only thing I've been truthful with him about," Cara retorted.

"That is your choice, although I think you'd be surprised at his response if you did tell him about your life with Constantinos. Yannis is not such an old-fashioned man to disdain a previously married woman."

"He's old-fashioned enough to live at home with his aunt and uncle and care what happens to their construction business."

"His uncle deserves to have his plans wrecked, since he never should have made them in the first place," Athena scoffed. "And Yannis has other irons in the fire anyway."

What did she mean about Yannis having other irons in the fire? Cara was about to ask when Athena grabbed her elbow. "Come. Walk me around the land."

The land was flat and easy for Athena to pass along. She muttered to herself, mostly imprecations against Yannis's uncle Gus. Cara didn't know the man well, but thought he'd been underhanded to go against a dead woman's wishes. She hoped Yannis didn't have the same questionable morality, although she couldn't imagine why that would be a problem. After all, they were just playmates for a summer fling.

Concentrating on her own thoughts and not paying attention to her steps, Cara stumbled. Fortunately she'd let go of Athena as she fell onto her hands and knees.

"Karoleena, are you all right?" Athena cried.

"Yes, yes, I'm fine." Cara looked down at the ledge of dirt she'd fallen off. They'd been walking on a higher part of the land and Cara had stepped into an indentation, not much lower than the rest, but enough to trip her up.

"As long as you are not hurt. Did you trip over something?" Athena brushed loose gravel and dust off Cara's knees, tsking as she went. "You are going to have some marks."

"The ground drops off here, so be careful." Cara wiped her palms clean on her denim shorts. Fortunately, there was no bleeding as the rocks had only scraped her skin.

Athena nodded and they went on, careful to avoid the drop-off. They came to an olive tree and stopped to rest in its shade. Athena looked back along the path they had taken and narrowed her eyes. "Do you see that, Cara?"

Cara stared at the sparse bushes and drooping trees that probably flowered in the spring. "It's very pretty, Athena. I can see why you wanted to build here."

She waved a hand. "No, not that—the lower ground you tripped on is a huge rectangle."

"Really?" Cara blinked and let her gaze travel along the path. It did appear to be a rectangular shape. She left Athena under the tree and walked the upper perimeter. "You're right!" she called. "It's almost as big as a football field." She continued to the end where the goalposts would stand. "There's a big mound up at this end. No, wait, I'll come help you."

Athena had pushed away from the tree and was speed-walking toward her. Cara met her halfway. "Careful, careful."

"Bah!" Athena ignored Cara's concern. "Show me what you saw." Cara followed as Athena hurried to eye the clump of shrubs raised up on a smaller rectangular mound. "Almost like an altar…" she mused.

"Did there used to be a church out here?" Cara asked. The *koura* or cathedral in Aphrodisias was several hundred years old and was in the center of the town. She couldn't see the locals coming all the way out into the hills to go to church.

"No." Athena shook her head. "Never a church…maybe a temple."

"A temple? To whom?"

The older woman turned and gave her a wide, calculating grin. "Aphrodite, of course." She burst into wild laughter. "*Kyria* Nomikou, you sly old lady, you left me Aphrodite's Temple, untouched and unexcavated. The archaeologists will swarm over this site like ants on honey. Oh, what can those foolish men say about this?"

Cara burst into laughter, as well. "You know Yannis and his uncle Gus will have plenty to say about this."

"I'll handle Gus, but I leave Yannis to you." She wiggled her thick brows suggestively. "Tell me one thing, *chriso mou,* and I promise not to tease you anymore. Is Yannis Petrides descended from Zeus? He looks like a man with a long lightning bolt."

Cara sputtered, her cheeks heating. Athena hooted with laughter. "Never mind, darling. Your face tells me everything I wanted to know."

"YANNIS, finish up in there! You're worse than the girls."

Yeah, right. Yannis had begun his shower a whopping five minutes ago. He gave himself a final rinse and shut off the water. Living with his uncle's family as if he were still a kid was starting to get on his nerves, but at least it was only for the summer until he went back to school.

He reached for a towel and started drying off. He didn't know how Niko could stand living with his mother year-round. Actually, he *did* know. Niko had free room and board and then just went to a hotel with a tourist girl if they wanted to have sex. Whereas Yannis, being the classy type, fondled his own tourist girl in the water at a public beach and then had rough, quickie sex with her on a cabana chair. Or against an olive tree in his grandfather's vineyard. He sighed. Maybe someday, they would actually have a bed. At least she'd enjoyed herself, despite his almost animal-istic response to her. Or maybe because of it?

He smiled at himself in the mirror and then reached for his razor and shaving cream. No point in marking Cara's delicate skin. He was about to lather up when his uncle banged on the door again.

"Now, Yannis!"

"Fine, fine!" He wrapped the towel around his waist and unlocked the door.

Uncle Gus rushed in. "About time. You look pretty enough as it is."

"Thanks," he muttered. He shoved his gear back into the cabinet and rinsed the lather down the sink.

His uncle looked over his shoulder into the mirror, his black eyes crafty. "That redhead who drove Athena Kefalas to the job site?"

"Yes?" He raised an eyebrow, willing to be just as crafty as Gus.

"You know her?" Gus was just toying with him now, he could tell.

"Niko introduced us. I've run into her a few times."

Gus smiled. "Did she move to Aphrodisias to start a construction company? Because the boys said she met you after work at the job site. Are you showing her the *ins* and *outs* of our business?" Gus chortled and slapped Yannis on the back.

Yannis gave him a sour look. How many more weeks did he need to live here? He couldn't wait to get back to Ohio where his neighbors didn't know who he was sleeping with and wouldn't care if they did.

His uncle got serious with some effort. "Look, Yannis, I'm not asking to be nosy."

No, he was asking because he was a dirty old man.

"I'm asking because if this girl is a friend of Athena's, then she might, you know, *know* things about Athena, like is she going to give us more trouble about our Belgian villa project?"

"I'm sure she will, Uncle. The heirs basically welshed on the deal she had with their grandmother, so she has plenty to complain about."

Gus threw up his hands. "Yeah, yeah, yeah." He didn't want to be bothered with the ethics of the thing. That was the trouble with Uncle Gus. Yannis had plenty of experience with the building trades, having been around them his whole life, but he'd never gotten used to certain cutthroat aspects of the business. At least Yannis wasn't as naive as his father had been——his trusting nature had cost their family almost everything.

"So will you do it? Will you ask this girl some questions?"

"What?" Yannis jerked his attention back to his uncle.

"You know, take her out, wine her, dine her, learn what Athena is up to. As a favor for your uncle. And for the company." He reached for his money clip and pulled out some euros. "Dinner on me."

"Well…" Yannis didn't need the money, but enjoyed being on the turnaround side of his uncle.

Gus frowned and pulled out a couple more bills and shook them in front of Yannis's nose. "Think of your aunt. Think of your cousins. Even if she is a redhead, you can spend *some* time with her."

Annoyed by his uncle's backhanded insult to Cara, Yannis grabbed the money. "I'll see what I can do."

"Good boy. Now get out. You don't want to be anywhere around here. I had goat stew for lunch that didn't agree with me."

Yannis fled.

"HELLO, STRANGER." Emma lifted her sunglasses and peered up at Cara from where she reclined on a low-slung chair. "Did you have trouble finding me?"

"Not with that hot-pink bikini." Emma was turning into a beach bunny and had developed a pale golden tan, spending the past few days at the beach when Cara was visiting or plotting with Athena. Her evenings and nights were spent with Nick, sometimes at the villa, but they had grown more considerate than their first time there. "But why are you way over here? The beach is pretty rocky."

"I didn't feel like swimming and there were too many kids over there. I was reading and their ball knocked the book right out of my hands." Emma pointed to a thick, brightly colored paperback sitting near her leg. "How is Athena doing?"

"Fine. She had me looking up phone numbers for archaeologists who might be interested in the possible temple compound." Cara unfolded her own chair and arranged her towel on top.

"How neat! But don't archaeologists need permission from landowners to dig?"

Cara shrugged. "I tried to tell her that, but insignificant details like that don't concern her." She sat and smoothed sunblock over her skin, which had also darkened slightly since their arrival. The light tan looked good with her turquoise bikini and aquamarine belly ring. Maybe she'd get a matching ankle bracelet. Emma was wearing her pink one today.

Cara settled into her chair and closed her eyes. They flew open as several drops of icy water landed on her bare stomach. "Yikes!"

Emma was leaning over her, shaking her water bottle onto Cara. "Yikes, yourself. You don't get a nap until I hear what the heck you've been up to with Yannis."

Cara felt a flush that couldn't be explained away by a sudden sunburn.

"Aha!" Emma crowed, setting down her bottle. "I knew he had it bad for you as soon as he saw you in the taverna. So have you and he…?" Emma made a vague, fluttering motion with her hands.

Cara grinned. "Yes."

Emma leaned over and hugged her. "Tell me everything, you sly girl. When was your first time? Was it romantic?"

"Well, we left the taverna that first night—"

"You naughty girl! I should dump this water over your head for keeping it a secret for a week. I thought you were spending your free time with Athena." She shook the bottle. "But I won't, as long as you give me all the details."

"After the taverna, he took me on a scooter ride along the coast." Cara sighed at the memory. "The moon was full and all the stars were out. The breeze was blowing our hair as we drove, and the night smelled of flowers."

"Ohhh…" Emma sighed, as well. "Then what?"

"I wanted to go for a walk on the beach, and then we decided to go for a swim—"

"A skinny-dip?" she asked eagerly.

"Yeah." Cara blushed again. "And there we were in the ocean, and one thing led to another and we wound up on a cabana lounge chair… Oh, Emma, he was so hot and wanted me so much. I just couldn't help myself. I've never done anything like that before." Yannis just blew away all her inhibitions. She'd gladly accepted the risk of discovery, but knew somehow he'd never let anything bad happen to her. She'd never felt so safe with a man.

Her friend's eyes had widened. "In the water and on the beach? I promise, I will never order one of those Sex on the Beach drinks without thinking of you." She giggled. "And I thought Nick and I were daring, doing it on the floor."

"Um, yeah." Cara would never, ever admit to Emma she'd been an unwitting witness to that precious memory. "So, I don't know. It's been less than a week, and I can't think of anything but him. Every time I leave him, I count how long until I see him again."

"Have you told him you were married before?"

"No way. We haven't had the 'talk about our past love lives' conversation yet." And that conversation would be a long time coming, if she had her choice. Talk about a good way to frighten off a guy—she could just imagine that scenario. *Guess what, sweetie? I was married to a Greek man before we met. Who? Con Constantinos, that rich guy—you might have seen photos of him and his mistress in the tabloids.* Cara shook her head. "How about you?"

"Cara, I barely have any past love life. We just talk about our jobs, a bit about our families."

"That sounds cozy. Is Nick properly impressed with your academic achievements?"

Emma's eyes shifted to the side. "Well…"

"What?" Was Emma embarrassed about her math ability?

"I told him I was training to be a math teacher." Her words rushed out. "I didn't mention the bit about grad school."

"Emma! Why on earth would you keep that a secret? You teach advanced theoretical mathematics to graduate students. You were voted Graduate Assistant of the Year three times." Cara pursed her lips. "Is Nick one of those barbarians who is intimidated by smart women?" Like Con?

"Of course not! It's just a welcome change to meet somebody who wants *me*, not my brain." She shoved out her lips in a pout. "I'm tired of being a math geek, Cara. I want to enjoy myself, not make a decent guy feel stupid because I have a college degree and he doesn't. I want to be a bimbo this summer. Why should they have all the fun?"

It was hard to disagree. Cara wasn't exactly winning prizes for Most Honest Summer Fling, either. "Being a bimbo is overrated—you have to spend too much time on your hair and clothes, too much time worrying about being skinny enough." Too much time in the bathroom trying to get skinny enough to recapture her husband's wandering attention.

Emma's face softened. "Suffering from bulimia wasn't your fault. The new research shows real imbalances in hormones and brain chemistry. You should be proud of yourself for getting help and getting better."

She shrugged, still uncomfortable with discussing her past. "So this summer, you can be the math teacher bimbo and I'll be the…" Who would she be? More to the point, who *was* she? And how was she supposed to tell Yannis who she was when she hadn't figured it out yet? "I'll be the American college student who's met a really nice, hot Greek guy for a sexy summer fling." At least that was part of the truth.

"Sounds good." Emma gave her a relieved smile.

Cara remembered she'd discussed Emma's education with Yannis the first night they'd gone out together, and made a mental note to ask him not to mention it to Nick. "Oh, Emma, I almost forgot. Your academic advisor left you a message on my cell phone."

She sat up and frowned. "Oh, pooh. Sorry about that, Cara. I only gave her that as an emergency number. What did Dr. Gaithers want?"

"She wants you to call or e-mail her back to discuss your progress so far this summer." Cara eyed her friend. You didn't have to be a math genius like Emma to add one budding tan, one promising summer affair and one dusty laptop to come up with how much progress Emma was making on her grad work.

Emma rolled her eyes and popped her sunglasses back on. "I'll send her an e-mail today—no, wait, Nick is getting out of work early and we're taking the ferry to Mykonos for the weekend."

"Really? Your first trip together, huh." So far, Emma and Nick had mostly gone out for dinner and then back to the villa for sex. "Mykonos is fun—a real party town. It was built by pirates for their mistresses."

Emma giggled. "Really?"

"Yep. One writer wrote several hundred years ago that the women on Mykonos were more noted for their beauty than their chastity."

"Kind of like us," Emma chortled. "And it's about time."

Cara laughed and reclined into her seat. The late-afternoon sun relaxed her almost to the point of sleep. She wasn't sure how long had passed before Emma exclaimed, "Oh, my gosh!"

"What? What?" Cara sat up and wildly looked around. Emma slammed her chair shut and tossed her gear into her bag.

"Nick's going to come pick me up in an hour and I need to shower and finish packing." She slipped on her cover-up and sandals and started hiking up to the road. "I'll see you late Sunday, okay?"

"Okay. Have a great time!" Cara called. Emma waved and then scurried off. Cara settled into her chair again, but noticed Emma's paperback in the sand. She'd just take it back to the villa for her.

Brushing off the cover, she raised her eyebrows at the metallic-gold title—*Sins of Summer*. Intrigued, she flipped to the first page and started reading. The third chapter was particularly juicy, the glamorous heroine lounging around her estate in the Hamptons, spying on the half-dressed, well-built gardener. The hunky horticulturalist was preening at his boss's rapt attention when a shadow fell over the pages and Cara squeaked.

"Sorry, Cara, I thought you heard me coming. I saw Emma at your place and she told me you were here." Yannis bent down and kissed her. He must have come from the job site since he wore his customary cotton T-shirt and work boots. Today he was sporting khaki carpenter shorts, his legs strong and brown under them. "My lazy crew actually finished their work early. Good book?"

"I guess." She marked the page with her finger, slightly embarrassed. "Emma forgot it earlier."

"Oh, right. Niko said they're going to Mykonos tonight. His aunt has a nice couch for her to sleep on there."

Cara stared at him in horror. "Emma is planning a romantic weekend, and Niko's having them stay at his aunt's house?"

"It's a big house," Yannis said innocently before bursting into laughter. "No, he did get a hotel room. Not as fancy as yours, but they probably won't catch bedbugs. I hope."

"Oh, you." Cara slugged him in the arm.

"Where did you leave off?" He plucked the book from her, his eyes widening. "I leave you to go to work for just a few hours, and you have to read this? I must not be doing my job to satisfy you."

"What? What?" Cara grabbed the book and looked at where his finger rested. The slinky heroine was seducing the gardener in the middle of the lawn. "I didn't get to this part yet."

Yannis read aloud over her shoulder, "'She licked her suddenly dry lips as he unzipped his shorts. His magnificent purple manroot bulged—'" He broke off. "Manroot? Is that what I think it is?"

Cara muffled her giggles unsuccessfully. "Exactly."

He shook his head and took the book from her. "All those years of studying English and I never learned that word before."

"Consider yourself fortunate."

"Skipping the manroot parts…" He grinned at Cara's

snort at his pun. "Ah, here we go. 'She was clad in the tiniest of bikinis, knowing his hot eyes would eagerly travel over her body—' How did his eyes get out of his body? Is that some American phrase?"

"No, just bad writing."

Yannis studied the book again. "'His callused finger traveled gently over her soft skin, as if amazed it was permitted to touch such lovely silkiness. He untied her bikini top and feasted his eyes on her bounteous mounds of pleasure.'"

Cara's giggles broke off when Yannis yanked the tie behind her neck, her top falling loose. "Yannis!" She pressed the cups against her breasts. "I didn't mean for *you* to feast *your* eyes."

"There's nobody around, and I want to see your bounteous mounds." He tugged the top free and tossed it to the sand behind him. "Show me, Cara *mou*. Then we can find out what happens next."

She slowly unfolded her arms, baring herself. She'd sunbathed topless years ago, but not recently; pale triangles of skin outlined the areas her suit usually covered.

"Nice, very nice." He nodded in approval and dropped the paperback on the sand. "But you'll burn quickly unless…" He picked up the sunblock and drizzled it over her breasts.

"Yikes, that's cold!" Her nipples immediately tightened, in reaction to him as much as the change in temperature.

"Not if you rub it in." With his hands he began massaging the cream into her skin.

She grabbed his wrist. "Yannis, I don't think we're supposed to do this here."

"What?" He gave her an innocent look. "Topless sunbathing is permitted on this end of the beach, and I'm just a good Greek host trying to keep a pretty tourist from getting sunburned."

Cara looked around. They were several hundred yards from anyone, being on the rocky end of the beach. She let go of his wrist and lay back on the chair. "Just so I don't burn."

"Of course." She squirmed on the chair as he took his time, his fingers leisurely slipping and sliding over her. "There's an art to this, you know."

"Oh, really?" Her breath was coming faster now.

"Yep." He nodded. "You have to be careful not to miss an inch of skin. Especially here." He caught one of her nipples between his slick thumb and finger and rubbed the peak. Cara's hips twitched. "If you were to get sunburned here, how would I suck on you?"

A moan escaped from her. "Yannis…"

"Shhh." He moved to her other breast, massaging and squeezing her. The ocean breeze cooled her skin, making her nipples even harder. "Roll over on your side."

She looked up at him in confusion.

"Face me." He grabbed her hip until she was lying on her recliner like a topless pinup model, her back to the rest of the beach.

"But, Yannis, I don't want to sunbathe anymore. Let's go back to my place. Emma will be gone by now."

"No, not yet. This first." Before she could protest, he drove a finger under the waistband of her bikini bottom and found her clit.

She tossed her head back as lust speared through her. He was slick from the lotion, and her juices made him even more slippery. She grabbed his forearm, intending to stop him, but he shook his head.

"Not yet. You need me right here, right now." He reached over with his free hand and flicked her belly ring.

"So sexy. This jewel is like an arrow on a map, pointing down to right where I want to be." He stroked her little knot of pleasure as it swelled under his finger. "Right here where you want me to be."

"Yes, Yannis," she panted. "Always."

He dipped into her passage and she contracted around him. "Do you remember when we were under the olive tree and I was licking you?" His expression was casual, as if she had just decided to roll over to chat with him, but his cock pressed hard against his fly and a droplet of sweat ran down his temple. "You were the sweetest thing I had ever tasted."

She groaned. "You, too," was all she could manage.

"Oh, yes. Your soft mouth on me drove me crazy, made me suck you harder. I only wished I could see your beautiful face, watched you crest and soften when you came."

Heat spread up into her cheeks at his sexy talk and his even sexier caresses.

"I'm going to take you home to your villa and soap you up in the shower. Your breasts." He stroked them, obviously enjoying how she shivered at his delicate touch. "Your ass." He cupped her there, pinching and squeezing. By then she was so aroused, she didn't protest at how anyone could see him. "And here, your soft copper nest. My cock wants to be *here*." He slipped his whole hand into her suit, working two fingers inside her with his thumb on her clit. "I'll spread your thighs wide on the bed and not let you up all weekend."

Cara bit her lip to hold back her cries, but his fingers just sped up. Her hips bucked on the lounge chair, making it squeak and sink deeper into the sand.

"Now, Cara *mou,* show me that beautiful expression I love to see, the expression that I alone can give you." He pinched her clit and she melted under his hands, her pussy wildly pulsing around his long fingers. He muffled her scream with a hard kiss, his own desire and frustration finally breaking free. He drove his tongue deep into her mouth, mimicking exactly what he planned to do to her once they were truly alone.

She clutched at his arms as the shock waves of her orgasm continued to ripple through her. He was her only anchor in the shifting sand, despite causing her torment. She broke away and gasped for breath. "Oh, Yannis, Yannis."

He pulled his hands free and she closed her eyes, slumping back on the chair. She felt a kiss pressed to her forehead and then heard the rustle of him undressing and the jingle of keys.

She turned her head with her last bit of strength and opened heavy lids. He had taken off his boots and shirt and set the contents of his pockets on top. "Yannis, honey, what are you doing?"

"Going for a swim."

"Oh." She sat up and groped for her bikini top. His blue gaze focused hungrily on her swaying breasts. "Maybe I should swim, too."

He shook his head. "Not unless you want me to strip off the rest of your suit and fuck you in the water. I'm so hard for you that I don't even care who sees."

"Oh." His blunt confession made a fresh wave of desire break over her. She shifted and licked her lips, trying to ease the renewed ache.

He groaned and swore in Greek. "Just…just…stay there. God, I hope the water's cold." He stood, his bikini briefs not disguising his arousal one bit. He sprinted to the surf and dived in. Cara thought she heard a yelp as he went underwater.

She rested on the chair, pleasantly drained. The heat of

the sun on her bare breasts was nothing compared to Yannis's touch.

After several minutes, Yannis climbed up the beach. When he saw she was still topless, he closed his eyes. "Get dressed so I can take you home. It's the last time you'll need clothes until Monday."

YANNIS RUSHED into his house and headed to his room to throw some toiletries and clothes into a bag for their romantic weekend alone at the villa. He hated to leave Cara even for a short time, but a toothbrush and some deodorant wouldn't be amiss.

He clattered downstairs to leave a note for his aunt not to expect him home, but found his uncle in the kitchen lighting a cigarette and rummaging in the refrigerator.

"Eh, look, it's the Invisible Man. Your auntie was beginning to wonder if you'd moved out without telling her." He wiggled his gray bushy eyebrows. "I told her I've been keeping you busy at the office."

"I've been busy at the job site, but we finished everything on your list. Tell Aunt Eleni I won't be home this weekend. You can call me on my cell phone if something comes up." Yannis plucked some olives from the dish his uncle held and headed for the door.

"Just a minute, young man." Gus waved his cigarette at Yannis. "I've been more than patient waiting for your report, but I need some information now. What did you find out from the American girl?"

Yannis wished he'd never accepted the old man's measly bribe. "I haven't found out anything. You can have your money back." He dug into his wallet to hand the wad of euros to his uncle. Unfortunately two condom packets fell out.

Gus eyed them with glee. "You're quite the man-about-town, Yannis. Maybe you should keep the money—just for supplies, if you know what I mean."

"First of all, Cara has not told me anything that Athena Kefalas hasn't told you straight to your face. Athena feels you cheated her out of the land and is no doubt plotting to get it back."

"I did not cheat anyone!" Gus's face reddened. "No signature, no deal. If you are going to be a builder, you are going to have to be more businesslike, Yannis."

"You mean ruthless," Yannis retorted.

"Bah! You are soft and sentimental like your father. That is why he chips stone in cold, rainy London and not here on Aphrodisias."

Yannis's face burned. "My father trusted his business partner. How was he to know that crook cooked the books for years?"

"He would have known if he had paid more attention to money. But no, your father is an *artist*." It wasn't a compliment. "He was tied up in his architectural sculptures and never noticed his partner charging obscene amounts of money to their clients and giving your father a pittance. And even worse, misfiling taxes? Your father is lucky he didn't go to prison for tax fraud like his partner did."

Yannis gritted his teeth. His parents had moved to London for a fresh start after that humiliating time, and his father now worked for a famous architectural restoration firm. "My father is an honest man."

Gus had caught the underlying sentiment. "And I am not? Does my concrete work chip a year after I lay it? Do my foundations sag and the walls crack? Have any of my buildings ever come down during an earthquake?"

"No," he muttered. "But I won't quiz Cara about her friend's plans. It's not right."

Gus shook his head. "Not everyone sees right and wrong with your moral clarity, Yannis. I hope the rest of us do not disappoint you someday when we fail to live up to your lofty standards."

10

"Put down that fruit and come give me some of your sweetness." Yannis snagged Cara around the waist and gave her a long kiss, slipping a hand inside her terry cloth robe. Since she hadn't bothered to throw on any clothing for the past two days, he easily found what he wanted.

Cara dropped the melon on the countertop as he pinched her nipple just the way she liked. His own robe gaped open to reveal his brown, muscular chest. "You are insatiable. We've barely left the bedroom since Friday." Now they were enjoying a leisurely Sunday afternoon. "Haven't you gotten enough?" Despite her teasing words, she nudged his robe open and found his erection with her hand.

"Never enough with you, Cara." He jolted his hips into her grasp. "Hmm, this table looks sturdy enough."

Just then the phone in the living room rang. Cara ignored it, instead enjoying Yannis's velvety skin sheathing hard, hot flesh. He buried his face in the crook of her neck and murmured sweet nothings in Greek to her. He was becoming more and more affectionate with her, and Cara wasn't used to that. It worried her for a minute, but then she realized that of course he'd be affectionate, considering how often they were naked together.

"Mmm, *latria mou, hara mou,* yeah, that's it," he muttered as she cupped his balls. Now she was his darling, his joy? Cara mentally pinched herself for letting anything distract her from his pleasure. He had given her so much pleasure that he deserved one just for himself. It was no sacrifice considering how sexy he was.

Yannis groaned, his sac tightening in her hand as he ripped open her robe. He frantically stroked every inch of her that he could reach—her breasts, her belly, her back, between her thighs—but she ignored the familiar heat since she could tell he was getting close. She ran her tongue around his ear. "I'm in charge this time, Yannis Petrides, and you're gonna beg me before you're done. You're a bad Greek boy to let an American girl lead you around by your cock." She squeezed his shaft and it jumped in her hand. "And your balls, too." She slipped a finger behind them and he moaned. "Maybe I should be really bossy and tie you to my bed and suck on you till you come." She stopped moving her hands on him. "Or not."

"Cara, please!" His voice was a hoarse cry. "Now, now…"

Close enough to count as begging. She literally manhandled him until he threw back his head, his neck tendons straining, roaring, "Yes, yes, yes…" He exploded into her grasp, clutching at her as his orgasm ripped through him. She felt strong and powerful as he gasped for air, Aphrodite bestowing a gift of love on a mere mortal.

Love? No, she had meant sex, not love. Or even affection, but not love. She released him and he rested against the heavy wood table, his chest heaving.

"Oh, Cara, what was that?"

"A little hostess gift." Or was she still pumping him for info?

He looked confused, but then again, wasn't she? They

cleaned up and tried again with the food. This time when the phone rang, Cara answered it.

"Hello?"

"Hello, darling." It was Athena, speaking in Greek. "I called in a few favors and found one of the university archaeologists over on Naxos. She is coming tomorrow to evaluate if the land was an ancient temple of Aphrodite."

Cara was careful to respond to Athena's Greek in English. "What? I thought you were joking. How can you know what it is after thousands of years just by looking at it?"

"Ah, you're speaking English. Is Yannis there?"

"Yes." He was gathering items for their snack as if he knew what he was doing in a kitchen.

"Well, looking at it *is* the archaeologist's job. She grew up on Naxos and has always been fascinated by the ancient temples to the goddesses. And she is applying for tenure!" Athena finished triumphantly.

"Great." An ambitious professor would be Uncle Gus's worst nightmare. "And what about the owners?"

"According to Greek law, antiquities are government property. Whatever might be underground there belongs to the people of Greece, so that is protected land until the archaeologist says it's empty."

"But you don't think that."

"Of course not. Something is there, and Dr. Aristides is the woman to find out."

"If you say so." Geez, what had happened to her uncomplicated summer of sunbathing and swimming?

"It is not I who says so, but the government." Athena's voice came out a bit sharper than usual. "Pass along this news to Yannis."

Cara sighed. Caught in the middle again. "Fine."

"Come meet the professor tomorrow at ten. Then we can plan our next step. Goodbye, Karoleena." Athena hung up, doubtless to avoid any more protests.

Yannis had finished slicing up the fruit and had found some goat milk feta cheese and brine-soaked black olives. He was quite handy in the kitchen. His mother must have taught him some basic skills. "That was Athena?" he questioned.

"Yes." She picked up the bottle of strong red wine and filled two glasses. A bit of wine from the romantic vineyard might make the news go over better, although she doubted it. "Let's eat on the terrace."

"In our robes?" He looked down with mock horror. "Someone might get the wrong idea."

"No, they'd probably get the right idea." She drank half her glass and refilled it. "Come on."

He followed her outside, where the roses grew overhead on an arbor, muting the June afternoon sun and giving them some shade. He pulled two chairs close together and set the platter on a small mosaic table between them. "Nice day."

"Do you want to go out?" She bit into the salty, slightly sour feta and followed with a melon chunk.

"Are you kidding?" He gestured to their surroundings with his wineglass. "For once, we have food, we have a bed, we have a shower with plenty of hot water for soaping each other up. Why would I want to leave?"

She laughed and picked up an olive. He caught her hand and sucked it into his mouth, deliberately swirling his tongue around her fingers. "If only we didn't have a phone…" he mused.

"Oh, yes, that." Cara took a deep breath. "Something came up in regards to the property she and your uncle are fighting over."

"I should have told you he made the same request as Athena—that I pass along any information I found out. But I figured Athena can tell him herself. She's not shy."

"No, Yannis. This is serious and could change everything."

"Yeah?" He sat up straight, his mellow mood melting away. "What is it?"

"It's a historical site."

He shrugged and relaxed. "The whole island is a historical site. Aphrodisias has been continually inhabited for the past seven thousand years, according to the archaeologists who wander through every so often."

"It will block your uncle's plans for the near future. Maybe permanently."

He narrowed his eyes. "What do you mean permanently? He's counting on this for his business. He could be in trouble if it doesn't go through." Yannis threw up his hands in frustration and jumped up to pace back and forth on the tiny balcony.

Cara sympathized, but she knew Athena was right. "There's a very good possibility that it was once the site of the temple dedicated to Aphrodite."

"Oh, come on. There have to be at least six or seven supposed sites of that temple. The whole island was dedicated to Aphrodite. Does that mean we throw everybody off the island and leave it for the goats?" He dropped into the wrought-iron chair and drummed his fingers on the table.

Cara shrugged. "There's some compelling evidence. The property has been in *Kyria* Nomikou's family for hundreds of years and passed down only through the women. Athena says the old lady used to claim she was a direct descendant of the priestesses of Aphrodite."

Yannis stared at her and burst out laughing. "Really? She admitted that?"

"Sure, why not?" His snickers were starting to get on her nerves.

"Cara, sweetheart, in the old days the priestesses of Aphrodite were mostly professional lovers, if you know what I mean."

"You mean hookers? Call girls? Ladies of the evening?" she said sweetly, and had the satisfaction of seeing him choke on his wine in surprise. He *did* know quite a bit of American slang. "After all," she continued, "Athena says most of the men on the island claim to be descendants of Zeus despite their puny lightning rods."

He winced. "And I thought she was this sweet old lady who baked great cookies."

"Apparently she has a broader set of experiences than either of us thought." She dropped into the chair next to him.

"I guess. She spent several years in Athens keeping house for that rich cousin of hers, Con Constantinos."

Hearing her husband's name was a surprise, but then Cara had an even more horrible thought. "But you're Athena's cousin, too. Are you related to that guy?"

"No." He shook his head. "Athena was related to him on her father's side, and she's related to me on her mother's." He laughed. "Too bad, eh? Then I might have inherited some money from him when he died. Athena got a bundle, but that American trophy wife of his got the lion's share according to Greek inheritance law. Boy, was the rest of his family pissed off." He poured more wine. "Although my aunt said she was a pretty blond girl, so she must have kept him happy."

Cara wanted to throw up. She'd been called worse than a trophy wife by Con's family, the tabloids and Greek so-called "entertainment" television, but hearing it from Yannis was the worst. She forced her numb lips to say, "I heard of him. Wasn't there something strange about how he died?"

Yannis shrugged, unaware he was tossing bombs into her lap. "He supposedly had a heart attack in his long-term mistress's arms. Kind of young, but according to my aunt Eleni, weak hearts ran in the family."

Weak hearts and weak characters, too. Yannis was absolutely right. Con had collapsed on top of former Greek ballet star and long-term lover Clio Papadopoulos. A little thing like marriage to Cara had not even been a bump in the road of their affair. Like most ballet dancers, Clio had been tiny and slender to the point of emaciation, obviously what Con preferred in women since he had tacitly encouraged her own insane weight control methods.

Cara grabbed a huge hunk of feta off the plate and bit some off, chewing angrily. She slowed down when she realized she wasn't even hungry. So why would she eat? To spite a dead man? She sighed and set the rest down. No more eating to stuff her emotions instead of her stomach. It was time to come clean to Yannis about her past with rich, successful, cheating Con Constantinos. But he continued before she could open her mouth.

"Yeah, Aunt Eleni loves all those gossipy, celebrity magazines. That's all she and her friends talk about when they get together for coffee. Who's marrying who, who's cheating on who, who's getting a divorce."

"Really? She follows that stuff so closely?" If that was true, Cara didn't dare tell Yannis she was Con's widow. If the paparazzi discovered she'd returned to Greece, Aphrodisias would become hell on earth with dozens of scooter-riding photographers chasing her, Yannis, Emma, Athena and anyone unlucky enough to know her. She'd been chased enough to be seriously frightened many times, she and her security detail even crashing their car once. Having such a relatively small population meant intense media scrutiny for anyone in Greece with any kind of celebrity status.

He laughed. "She's always asking Athena what it was like to work for a real-life Greek shipping tycoon, but Athena never says anything."

Thank goodness for Athena's tight lips. "I don't suppose you know what happened to the American wife after he died?"

He shrugged, losing interest in what was obviously old news to him. "Apparently she went back to America a very wealthy woman. But that was several years ago. Hey, are you okay? You look kind of pale."

She touched her forehead, which had started to hurt from stress and upset. Hearing her previous life in Greece reduced to its sordid skeleton made her want to cry. American blond bimbo marries rich Greek shipping magnate, inherits half his money despite the loud protests of his relatives, and takes off for the States with her loot. Add to that the prospect of the paparazzi hounding her until she either fled again or went into hiding, and it was no wonder she'd had enough.

"I have a headache all of a sudden. I used to get migraines before, but I haven't had one in a long time."

"A migraine?" He stood up in alarm. "Do you have medicine for it? I can go get it."

"No, I don't have anything." She'd thought she'd had something with Yannis, but her past still interfered.

"Come here." He helped her to her feet and then swung her up into his arms.

"Yannis…" she protested, but he carried her into her bedroom where he undid her robe and helped her into a largely unused cotton nightgown. His touch was kind, but not sexual, his eyes full of concern.

"Climb in bed and I'll get you something for the pain."

"Okay." She blinked. The afternoon sun was sparking little haloes in her vision, and he shut the shades.

"I'll be right back, Cara *mou*. Just close your eyes and try to rest." He dropped his own robe and dressed.

"Yannis…" The lump in her throat was nearly blocking her voice. "I'm sorry."

"For what?" He bent and kissed her forehead. "You didn't give yourself a headache." He let himself out and she heard his steps clatter down the stone stairs.

But she *had* given herself a headache, one that had started when she met Con and had never totally gone away.

Yannis hurried back to the villa with Cara's medicine. He quietly pushed open her bedroom door and found her sleeping. Despite the dim light, the tear tracks on her face were visible. His heart twisted. His poor Cara, in so much pain it made her cry.

He filled a glass with water and sat next to her on the bed. "Cara, I have your pain medicine."

She slowly opened her eyes and to his dismay, they filled again with tears. "Oh, Yannis."

"No, no, it's okay. The pharmacist says this will help." He fumbled the pills, but managed to hand her the right dosage. "Take these."

She sat up and swallowed the pills. "Don't leave me, Yannis."

"I won't." He couldn't. Maybe not ever. Not ever? His thoughts echoed through his head as he kicked off his shoes and lay down next to her.

He hadn't planned any of this when he'd come back to Aphrodisias for the summer. He'd wanted construction experience, some money for school and a summer at the beach.

Instead, Cara had burst into his life, first in the alley then again at the taverna, her personality as fiery as her luxurious hair. She had led him a merry chase before letting him seduce her—or had it been the other way around?

He grinned to himself. It didn't matter. What mattered was he couldn't get enough of her—had a hard time keeping his hands off her. More than that, he wondered what would happen once the summer ended.

He'd been too busy during school to date seriously, not letting his social life interfere with his career ambitions. But if there were a woman who could distract him, it was Cara.

He stroked her tumbled hair, hoping her headache started to feel better.

Her breathing slowed as she fell back asleep. He closed his eyes and inhaled the scent that was uniquely Cara's, a blend of sun, sea and her own honey-sweetness. As for what would happen to them after their Greek summer together, only the Fates could say.

"COFFEE, *chriso mou?*" At Cara's nod, Athena set a cup down on the small glass table in the garden behind her house. "I can fix you some lunch if you are hungry," she offered. The sun was high overhead, but they sat under an arch of purple and white bougainvillea shading much of the rays.

"Maybe in a little bit." Cara sipped her coffee and stared at Athena's garden. She'd slept late, not even waking when Yannis must have left the villa to go to work. What a Monday. She still felt slightly hungover from her migraine medicine, but the sound of water trickling from the copper wall spigot of the blue-and-white tiled fountain smoothed her fuzzy nerves.

Athena settled into the chair next to her. Today she was wearing a more modern outfit of khaki slacks and a white embroidered blouse and a sturdy pair of walking shoes. "Dr. Aristides arrived this morning on the ferry from Naxos. She brought some students and Demetria drove all of us to the temple property. We stopped for you, but Emma said you had a sick headache yesterday, so we let you sleep. The professor and the students are still there for a preliminary survey."

"What does the professor say?" It had to be good news for Athena judging from the broad smile on her face.

"'Very promising,'" Athena quoted. "She says the site is remarkably similar to a temple excavated down on Crete. That temple turned out to be gigantic and quite a find. Dr. Aristides will make a report to the Hellenic Ministry of Culture as soon as she finishes a preliminary assessment."

Cara stretched out her legs. The acidic coffee wasn't sitting well on her empty stomach. "What does this mean for your museum and Gus's villa project?"

"They are both on hold," Athena admitted. "A bit of a Pyrrhic victory," she said, referring to the ancient Greek battle where the victors were harmed just as much as the losers.

"You knew that would happen when you called in the experts," Cara replied.

"True." Athena reached over and pinched off a brown bloom. "But it is worth it to see the expression on that old goat's face when he finds out. Serves him right for being so underhanded." She smiled, her cheeks wrinkling into a fine net of lines. The tradition of revenge was alive and well on Aphrodisias.

"Well, the archaeologist has thrown enough monkey wrenches into the underhanded property sale. Even if Gus could buy the land, the excavation will take years, and what rich tourist wants to buy a fancy house next to a dig site? Your museum is in a much better position to eventually buy the land and incorporate any archaeological findings into its exhibits."

"Wonderful idea, Cara." Cara's stomach growled. "Eh, you haven't eaten yet today, have you?" Athena leaped up and soon returned with a tray of *spanikopita* squares, grilled bread topped with olive oil and salt along with the ubiquitous Greek coffee cups. "Eat, eat."

"Don't worry, Athena. I'm not going back to what I used to do." To prove her point, Cara bit into a *spanikopita*. The crispy phyllo pastry blended perfectly with the creamy feta cheese and mellow spinach.

"I know that, darling. You are not the same woman you were then. I think Greece has finally been good for you. And good to you."

Cara nearly choked on a stray phyllo crumb. "That's only because no one knows who I am—"

"Who you *were*," Athena rapidly corrected. "And that was never the true you in the first place."

"But Yannis knows about me." The remnants of her headache stirred at the memory.

Athena raised a brow. "Really? When did you tell him?"

"I didn't. I mean, we were talking about how you used to live in Athens and then he mentioned Con and his American widow."

"Oh. I see." Athena was obviously disappointed Cara hadn't taken the chance to come clean with Yannis. "So you told him nothing. You did not tell him how you left home at eighteen to get away from your parents' battles and worked your way up to sailing ships for the richest, most powerful people in the world. How you would have captained your own ship in just a few years had Con not swept you off your feet."

Cara shook her head. "I still don't know why Con singled me out. If I'd had my thinking cap on instead of being dazzled, I would have realized he was just playing me for a fool."

"Stop." Athena raised her hand. "You were everything Con wished he could be but wasn't—cheerful, humorous and liked for yourself, not your money."

"I never had any." Cara could finally muster up a weak smile.

"Constantinos had plenty of money, but he knew it was not enough. He envied the qualities that attracted him to you in the first place." Athena shrugged. "For him, it was easier to drag you down to his own misery rather than lift himself up."

"Really?" Con had envied *her?* Sturdy, redheaded sailor Cara?

"Really." Athena sipped her coffee. "I knew him since he was a boy. His father ignored him and his mother spoiled him—Con swung between thinking he was nothing and thinking he could do no wrong. Never any balance."

Cara sat back in her chair as she stared at a fat bumblebee drinking from a purple bloom. "Oh, Athena, why didn't he tell me any of this? I might have been able to do something to help."

She raised a thick dark brow. "What could you do? You could not starve away your spirit and give it to him, although he was willing to have you try. My darling, only *Theos* above can make a person whole, and Con didn't bother asking Him for help."

"I did," she admitted.

Athena captured her hand and gave it a squeeze. "As did I. But you know Greek men—they are stubborn as the goats and hard as the marble and nothing can make them change. What's done is done, *chriso mou*. You must look to the future, not the past. And your future is maybe here on Aphrodisias, eh?"

"You mean Yannis. I seem to have a tendency to fall for your cousins, Athena."

Her black eyes sharpened like a hawk that had spotted her prey. "So you have fallen in love with young Yannis."

"Love?" Cara clutched her *spanikopita*, feta and phyllo crumbs littering her lap.

"Yes, *love*. What is so bad about loving Yannis? He is a good boy, kind to that gossipy aunt and crook of an uncle." Athena helped herself to the grilled bread.

Cara jumped to her feet, food bits falling to the ground. "Yannis and I don't know each other well enough to even think of the word *love*. When I said I was falling for Yannis, I was just referring to our, um…"

"Passionate summer affair?" Athena interjected in a dry tone.

"Yes, that." Cara fought back a blush at the older woman's phrasing.

"Ah. And of course, you are a sophisticated woman who can have affairs of the body, but not of the heart. A woman who is only out for a hot time in the sack, as you Americans call it."

"Athena!" Cara just knew her face flamed as red as her hair.

"Pah!" Athena spat out. "You lie—not only to me, but to yourself."

"I am not lying," Cara insisted. "Yannis and I could never be in love, not once he knows who I am. He already thinks the worst of me—that I was a blond American bimbo who took half of Con's money—"

"You are no bimbo and Greek law stipulates that a widow without children inherits half the husband's estate. You know that. And by not telling Yannis important things about you, you have taken away his choice to decide who or what you are. You, of all people, who just now wished you had known more about your husband's past."

Cara sighed and slumped into her chair. "I should leave Greece before anyone gets hurt. I've only been dating him a few weeks—if I go back to Michigan now, he will have plenty of time to find somebody else to date this summer."

But the idea of Yannis embracing a sultry Greek beauty or statuesque Scandinavian jolted her stomach and almost startled a cry from her mouth. What if Athena was right? But she couldn't love Yannis after only a few weeks— could she? Athena compressed her lips so hard they vanished, and Cara could tell she was fighting back a retort. But when she did unclamp her mouth enough to speak, it wasn't what Cara expected. "Run away if you must, but at least stay for the big feast."

"What big feast?"

"Yannis's name day feast is Sunday, June 24, the Nativity of Agios Ioannis Prodromos, St. John the Baptist. Despite your merely casual feelings for Yannis, you would disappoint him greatly if you missed it. You know name days are much more important than birthdays here."

Cara did know that, and the Nativity of St. John the Baptist was a major holiday on Aphrodisias.

Athena continued, "His aunt and uncle are throwing a big party for him, and we are all invited."

"We are? Still?" Cara lifted an eyebrow. Athena and Gus were still tussling over the possible temple property.

"Of course!" She gave a belly laugh. "What's a Greek party without arguments? Everyone would fall asleep from boredom. Besides, you can meet his aunt Eleni, my cousin. She's a nice girl, even if all she thinks about is her hairdo, gossip magazines and what to cook for that bum of a husband. But she takes good care of your Yannis."

"He's not *my* Yannis," Cara pointed out yet again.

"Well, I don't see him trying to belong to anyone else, so whatever you do to the boy is certainly working."

The blood rushed to her face yet again. "Athena!"

"Ach, again with the blushes. Listen, *chriso mou,* I was married for twenty-five years and widowed for twenty. When we all lived in Athens, what do you think I did on my weekends off?"

Cara had never really thought about it. "Um, you wove tapestries?"

Athena roared. "I've never heard it called *that* before." She patted Cara's cheek. "No, my dear. I had lovers."

"Lovers?" As in plural?

"Of course. I did not die when my husband did, and there are plenty of kind, tender men who have lost their own spouses but do not plan to remarry." Athena gazed into the garden, a secret smile crossing her face. "So instead of wooing with a promise of marriage, they must woo with their skills in the bedroom."

Cara tried not to shudder, but it was as if her own grandmother was discussing her sex life. "Yannis is not wooing me."

Athena snapped back to the present. "You do not think so? Emma tells Demetria he brings you aspirin when you are sick, fixes food for you, takes you on long, long, *long* drives out into the country—" she wiggled her brows knowingly "—and you think this is not wooing? What do you want him to do—serenade you under your balcony with a bouzouki?" She broke into a famous Greek love song that of course ended with heartbreak and tragedy.

Cara wanted to pinch her. "You see? You see? Even the love songs know what's going to happen if I stay. I don't want to be wooed. I just want to go back to Michigan before anyone gets hurt." Especially her. Maybe she should leave as soon as possible, even before Yannis's name day. The next ferry for the mainland left Saturday, and she could be on it.

"Do you worry about Yannis being hurt or yourself?" Athena eyed her closely, as if guessing at her whirlwind thoughts. "Who will be hurt if you stay, and who will be hurt if you go?"

Cara made a helpless motion. It was too much to consider.

"Okay, okay, I do not mean to bully you. Maybe you need a break to clear your mind?" Athena thought for a minute and snapped her fingers. "Ah! The perfect thing."

"What?" she asked warily.

"My cousin Stavros owns a bus and drives tourists out to the more remote parts of the island. Let him show you the real Aphrodisias, the wild Aphrodisias."

"Why can't I drive myself?"

Athena shook her head. "Easy to get lost out there, have a flat tire. Stavros would be happy to do this for you. I'd go with you, but the roads are too rough for me." She grabbed her hip and winced, Cara thought, a bit theatrically.

"Fine. What is it, a half-day tour?"

"Exactly. How about Friday?"

"Friday, Emma is going on a day trip to Santorini. I guess Niko is showing her the remnants of the volcano there."

"Niko, eh?" Athena rolled her eyes. "That boy would date a goat if it wore a blond wig."

"Athena…" Cara had had much the same thought, but had never voiced it from loyalty to her friend.

"Your friend is much too beautiful and smart for him. And his mother…" The older woman shuddered. "She makes Jocasta look like a disinterested mother."

Cara snorted. Jocasta was the mother of the mythological King Oedipus and the inspiration for Oedipal complexes everywhere.

"And Emma, does she know you're considering leaving?"

"No, I haven't discussed it with her, but if I do go, I'll make arrangements to pay for the rest of her summer here."

"And you think she will use your money to stay when you go?"

Cara sighed. "No, I suppose not."

"Of course not. She is a good friend to you, and she will leave when you leave."

"Athena…" Cara could feel the guilt sweeping over her. Running away was bad enough, but to drag her friend with her?

"Eh, not to worry, Karoleena. Didn't you say Niko was distracting Emma from her schoolwork? It will do her good to get away from him."

"I don't like to manipulate my friends that way, Athena."

Athena's black gaze slid away from hers and she busied herself with stacking the appetizer plates. "Emma will work things out for herself. But let Stavros take you on a nice calm trip into the heart of Aphrodisias. The goddess will help you know what to do, especially if you ask her."

As far as Cara's love life was concerned, Aphrodite would either shake her head in disgust or hold her nose at how bad Cara was stinking things up. Cara didn't see how visiting the deserted interior of the island would help, but a half day out in the sticks would make little difference. "Okay, one short trip with Stavros. Then I have to go."

Athena bent down to kiss her on the cheek. "Stavros will show you a new side of Aphrodisias you've never seen."

EMMA KNOCKED on Athena's blue door and Demetria opened it. "Emma!" Demetria swept her into a big hug and cheek-kiss. "You just missed Cara. She is going to the beach for some fresh air."

"Is she feeling better?" Emma had worried over Cara's pale face and puffy eyes this morning.

"Nothing a snack and some coffee couldn't help. Eh, you want something to eat?" Demetria overrode Emma's polite refusals and shepherded her toward the kitchen.

Athena was talking on the phone in the hallway, not quite yelling at someone. Athena started slightly to see Emma and then she grinned. She hung up and Demetria said something to her in Greek.

"English, please, Demetria. It's rude to speak Greek in front of our American guest."

Demetria snorted. "Fine. What did Stavros say?"

"Yes, naturally. Especially when I told him I'd tell his mother if he didn't do it."

Emma looked between them, confused. Demetria wore a long-suffering look on her face, while Athena's expression could only be described as triumphant.

"If you're in the middle of something, I can just go meet Cara at the beach…" she offered, her dislike of conflict kicking in.

"No, no!" Athena caught her elbow with a surprisingly strong grip. "In fact, I need you to do a favor for me, as well. Come into the kitchen, and I'll tell you how you can help our friend Cara."

Curiosity won out over caution, and Emma let herself be towed into the kitchen like a rowboat on the ocean. She just hoped she wouldn't get pulled into a whirlpool.

"CARA?" Emma approached her friend, who was lying on the couch reading an actual novel in Greek. She didn't know Cara could read Greek, as well as speak it.

Emma was impressed. She could read individual letters thanks to her mathematical training, of course, but putting them all together was a totally different skill.

"Yes, Emma?" Cara looked up from what appeared to be a paperback romance. Perfect summer reading, even if in another alphabet. Previously, Cara had always disdained romance novels, saying they raised unrealistic expectations of what men were actually like. Emma had been sad to hear that, so Cara's change of mind was a good sign.

Emma sat next to her. "Are you enjoying our trip?"

Cara frowned, puzzled. "Sure. Are you?"

"Absolutely." Shoot, she wasn't doing this right. She wasn't tricky like Athena, but she'd promised the older woman to help out Cara. "I mean, is Greece okay for you?"

"Emma, why do you ask?" Cara closed the book and set it on the coffee table.

"Athena said you had some unpleasant times associated with Greece."

"Oh." Cara sighed and sat up. "What else did she say?"

Emma looked away and fidgeted. "That was about it."

"Right." Cara gave her a half grin. "Well, remember when I told you I was married before?"

"Yeah, that was a surprise." She thought she'd known Cara pretty well until then.

"My husband was a Greek guy. We lived in Athens for a few years."

Emma blinked several times. So that was how Cara understood Greek so well.

"His name was Constantine, and he was so charming, really smooth. At least until right after the wedding. Then Prince Charming turned into a frog. No, not a frog—frogs are kind of cute—a slug."

"I'm really sorry he didn't treat you well, Cara. When did you divorce him?"

Cara tipped her head and studied Emma. "Athena really didn't tell you everything, did she?" Without waiting for an answer, she continued. "I only discovered that Constantine actually had a heart when it gave out as he was fu— ahem, boinking his mistress. The scandal was all over Europe."

"He died? As he was, um…" Emma clutched her own chest in shock. She didn't know what was more horrifying—the actual death of Cara's husband or the sordid circumstances. "Wow, Cara, I am so, so sorry." She pulled Cara into a swift hug, patting her springy hair. "And yet here you are in Greece. You are a brave woman to come back again and face your past—"

"Emma." Cara's voice vibrated against Emma's shoulder. "Emma, I can't breathe."

"Oh, sorry." She let go, and Cara sucked in a deep breath. Emma had a horrible thought. "Cara, are you using up all your inherited money to pay for our trip?"

Cara flopped back onto the couch and guffawed. "Constantine was one of the ten richest men in Greece. Greek law dictates that childless widows inherit half the estate. So you see before you, sweet Emma, one of the richest women in Greece."

"No!" Emma's jaw dropped.

"Oh, yes. You know the old saying, 'If you marry for money, you earn every penny'? I married Con for love, but wound up paying through the nose." She looked away, obviously lost in unpleasant memories.

Emma's stomach contracted. Their vacation of a lifetime was subsidized by Cara's pain and heartache. "Yannis never mentioned any of this to Nick."

Cara's head whipped around from where she'd been staring into space. "Yannis doesn't know, and you and I aren't going to tell him. Do you know how awkward it is for a regular guy to date a superrich woman? Everyone assumes he's a gigolo and she's bribing him for sex."

"Oh, please, Cara, anyone can tell that's not true," Emma scoffed.

"Remember that Scandinavian princess who married her handsome, younger bodyguard? The paparazzi called them 'the Princess and her Pauper' and calculated how much money he would earn every time they had sex."

"That's awful." Emma couldn't imagine what kind of people would do something like that.

"The paparazzi would love to get photos of Yannis and me and write lies about us." Cara gave her a crooked smile. "You could pay off your student loans easily if you let them know I was back in Greece dating a cute guy."

"Forget it," Emma retorted. "I'll teach algebra to sixth graders before I betray a friend."

"And does Nick still think you're a middle school math teacher?"

Emma picked at the fringe on the couch's woven throw. "Well, yeah."

"Why haven't you told him?" This time, Cara's tone was curious, rather than condemning, so Emma thought first instead of being defensive.

"I guess I was tired of all the preconceived notions about math geeks, all the high expectations I carry throughout the school year. My professors don't mean to pressure me so much, but then they brag about me to their colleagues at other schools. And when I present at symposiums or write journal articles, I can just feel everyone waiting for me to fail. Nick, well…" She shrugged her shoulders. "He doesn't expect anything of me except to enjoy myself. It's a nice change."

"Emma, I had no idea you felt that way." Cara touched Emma's hand. "You should have said something."

"Like you told me about being one of the richest women in Greece?" Emma felt an embarrassed flush creep up her face. "And I made a big deal over treating you to that bikini when you could buy two of everything in the shop."

Cara squeezed her hand, startling Emma. Cara was a wonderful friend, but definitely not touchy-feely. Emma was always the one who initiated hugs and comforting pats. "Emma, you were the first person in a long time to buy me a gift out of the goodness of your heart." Cara's blue eyes filled with tears. "No strings attached, no expectations except to enjoy myself."

Emma's eyes blurred, as well, as Cara echoed her previous sentiments. "You and I, what a pair."

Cara nodded and swiped her eyes with the backs of her hands. "I know. It's like being back in Greece is stripping away all the bandages I slapped on myself over the years. I don't know how much more I can take before I'm completely raw." She shivered despite the warm evening air blowing through the French doors.

"Yannis would help you heal, I just know it."

Cara sat up straight, looking alarmed. "Swear to me you

won't tell him this stuff. He doesn't need to get dragged into my mess for what's only some summer fun."

"You should tell him at some point."

"Like you told Nick all about yourself?" Cara's moment of weakness was obviously over.

"Okay, Miss Smarty-Pants, let's make a deal. I'll tell Nick about my doctoral work if you tell Yannis about your late husband and your money."

"They'll knock each other over racing to get away from us," Cara warned.

"If they do, then good riddance!" Emma declared. "We deserve better. So do we have a deal for this week?"

Cara hesitated. "Leave that up to me, Emma. I'll figure out when."

"Okay, Cara. I promise. But I think Yannis would understand."

Cara frowned at her, and Emma subsided. Cara had potential happiness with Yannis within her grasp, but was afraid to reach out for it, thanks to a dreadful marriage. And all Emma had to do to help was go along with Athena's plan.

Any guilt about deceiving Cara flew out the arched, whitewashed window. That horrible husband of hers! He certainly hadn't deserved Cara's love and trust.

Emma shook her head. No wonder Cara was gun-shy, even with such a nice guy as Yannis. Nick couldn't say enough good things about him, and you'd have to be blind to miss how Cara looked at him, and vice versa. But she knew if she pressed the subject, Cara would just close up on her. "So, Cara, tell me about your paperback."

Cara glanced down at the forgotten book on the table. "Oh, yeah, it's called *Naked Model,* and it's lots of fun. Here, let me translate the good parts for you."

"Oooh." Emma sat on the couch next to Cara and folded her leg under her as she listened to her friend read.

Emma didn't think Cara realized how wistful she sounded as she read the falling in love parts aloud. But that was okay. Soon she and Yannis would realize they were meant for each other, even if they did need a little nudge from Emma and Athena.

Y ANNIS TAPPED on Cara's door after work and immediately swept her into his arms. She opened her mouth eagerly to his and clung to him as if she were stuck in an Aphrodisian riptide. He pushed her inside the villa and eagerly dipped his tongue into her honeyed mouth, her luxuriant hair caressing his cheeks.

He finally lifted his head to say, "Let's go to bed."

Instead of agreeing, Cara stepped away from him. "Yannis, I have something to tell you." She looked nervous, which was unusual for her. "This is so hard to say." She hugged her arms around herself.

He moved to hug her but she jumped back. "Okay, Cara." He lifted his hands. "You can tell me anything." Unless…was she breaking up with him? He really didn't want to hear *that*. He shoved his hands into his pockets. "If you don't want to go out with me anymore…" he began.

"No, not that. It's something else." She looked pale and kept clutching nervously at her waist. Was it possible? He rapidly counted back. Just a few weeks since they had begun making love together.

"Are you…" He gestured vaguely at her middle and trailed off. "Are we, um, expecting?"

"What?" Her eyes grew wide with shock. "Expecting a baby? No, of course not! Geez, Yannis."

"Okay, okay," he backpedaled, a weird sense of disappointment dogging him. Not that he had wanted to cause an accidental pregnancy, but still…the image of a little girl or boy with bright blue eyes and red-tinged dark curly hair lurked in the back of his mind. Yannis Petrides, who didn't even want the responsibility of a goldfish, mooning over babies? He rubbed his face. What was going on with him?

Her dry laugh surprised him. "After that notion, maybe my bit of information won't be so horrifying. Come sit before you fall over." Yannis sat next to her on the sofa, still anxious to hear what she had to say.

She took a deep breath. "Yannis, I was married before."

Well, that wasn't what he'd expected to hear. His Cara had been someone's wife? Been in his bed?

The words spilled from her now that she'd started. "I met him when I was very young, he was several years older and swept me off my feet and I loved him, but he didn't really love me back and it ended badly for both of us…" She trailed off, her shoulders slumping.

How could the man *not* love Cara? Outrage straightened Yannis's spine. She was utterly lovable. What if the fool realized what he'd lost and came after her again? Yannis wouldn't step aside for any man. "Where does he live now?"

She looked uneasy again. "He had a heart attack two years ago and died. Yannis, I'm a widow."

A widow? The only thought that passed through his stunned brain was that Cara was the sexiest widow he'd ever seen.

WITH HIS WIDE EYES and gaping mouth, Yannis reminded Cara of a fish that had accidentally jumped onto her ship's deck. "Yannis?" she asked cautiously.

"A widow?"

"Yes. I normally wear a lot of black." Her lame joke made him frown.

Cara walked to the balcony doors for some fresh air. Her honesty had gone over like a lead balloon. Well, better she find out his true colors now rather than later, when she'd gone and fallen in love with him.

Love?

"Cara?"

She nodded silently, still facing out over the town. It was that quiet, hot time of day when only the tourists wandered the streets and the locals were all home in bed for their afternoon nap, either sleeping or doing other things. Things she could be doing with Yannis, if it weren't for her conscience.

"Do you have children?"

Longing and loss slammed into her. Oh, she'd wanted them, but her poor body had known better. "No. If I had children, I would be with them, not fooling around all summer."

He came up next to her and took her shoulders. "Fooling around? Is that what you think this is?"

She looked up into his angry face. Good—anger she could deal with, having had plenty of experience with that.

"What else?" She forced herself to shrug, lifting his hands off her. So she'd be heading back to Michigan sooner than she thought. There was no way she'd tell him the full extent of her humiliation and notoriety. Yannis would pity her, and she didn't want his pity.

"What else?" he echoed. "Yeah, well, I guess you had some lost time to make up for, right?"

"Right." What she hoped was a smile curved her lips. "You're okay with that, aren't you, Yannis? My husband—" geez, she hated to refer to Con as that "—my husband was older and more interested in other things—" like his mistress "—so we rarely spent any time together."

"You should have told me before," he snapped. "I hate liars. I guess Athena and the whole rest of the island already know, and I am the last one."

"No, only Athena and Emma. Not Nick, not your uncle, if that makes you feel better."

He jerked his arm into the air in a typically Greek gesture of impatience. "It doesn't."

Another petulant Greek man to deal with? She didn't need that. "What's done is done. What are you going to do about it?"

"I don't know!" He was steaming mad.

"Then you should go until you decide."

That threw him for a loop. Greeks were used to shouting out their differences until they either got into a fistfight or made up. "I go, then! You think about anything else you forgot to tell me and I may listen. Or not." He strode to the door and noisily closed it behind him.

Cara hastily stepped back from the balcony so Yannis couldn't see her watch him hop on his scooter and roar away.

Another man gone. Did Cara have the knack or what?

11

CARA SHOULDERED her backpack and found the bus Athena had described waiting in the small ferry dock parking lot. The bus was painted in the cheerful blue-and-white colors of the Greek flag overlaid with the ever-present summer dust. She peeked in the open door.

"Stavros?" she inquired of the man in the driver's seat.

"Eh, you must be Miss Cara." Stavros looked like a Greek tourism poster, barrel-chested and with a luxurious black mustache. "Welcome to my bus. I take good care of you, or else Athena…" He shuddered theatrically and then gave a big belly laugh.

Cara laughed, as well, her first since her argument with Yannis. She hadn't heard from him for three days and hadn't called him, either, despite Emma's urging. She wasn't going to chase after a man who obviously wanted to stay away from her.

She and the driver chatted for a few minutes, Stavros showing her pictures of his plump wife and good-looking children, who would be finishing the Greek version of high school in the next couple years. Cara made a mental note to expand her secret scholarship fund to include his children.

"Okay, we go." He slammed the bus door and turned over the ignition, the bus roaring to life after a couple false starts.

Cara looked around. She was alone on the bus. "Stavros, where is the rest of the tour?"

Stavros shrugged. "We pick them up in a couple kilometers, miss."

"Oh. All right." Cara fell into a vinyl seat as Stavros gunned the bus forward. They jolted through town for a few minutes until Stavros yanked the wheel to the side and stopped at a corner near the swimsuit shop. He flipped open the door.

"Eh, come on up," he called to someone standing on the sidewalk.

A voice called in Greek, "Stavros, come into the office to talk about your remodeling. Aunt Eleni sent pastries again today."

Instead of a busload of tourists, Cara saw a familiar black head ascend the steps. "Yannis?" Cara leaned down.

"Cara?" He ran up the stairs into the bus. "What are you—oof!" Stavros stomped on the accelerator and Yannis staggered into the aisle. Fortunately he hadn't fallen out the still-open door.

Yannis pulled himself into the seat across from Cara and berated Stavros for his reckless driving before turning to Cara. "What are you doing here?" he repeated, looking suspiciously from Stavros back to her.

She couldn't very well say Athena was sending her on a pilgrimage to ask the goddess Aphrodite for help with her screwed-up love life. Cara figured love pilgrimages were off the itinerary, since she was officially swearing off men for the rest of her life. Was there an organization in Greece for not-quite-virginal vestal virgins? "Athena's sending me on a tour so I can see the interior of the island." Before Cara left on the ferry for Mykonos tomorrow, not that Athena knew she was leaving. She'd been careful to keep her reservations a secret from Emma, as well, who was still madly in love with Nick. Cara had paid rent for the rest of the summer and planned to leave a nice envelope of euros for her friend to use.

"A bus tour?" He looked puzzled. "I would have taken you anywhere you wanted."

That was the problem. He would have, but that would mean she would spend more and more time with him, and never want to leave him.

"Well, I know you're busy with your uncle's projects…." Her sentence drifted off as she realized that most likely wasn't the case.

He raised a cynical eyebrow. "Not as busy as I would have been if that land wasn't covered in a swarm of grubby archaeology students."

Cara nodded. Any kind of development was on hold until the archaeologist submitted her official report to the antiquities commission. "So you were waiting on the corner for a bus ride?"

"Athena said Stavros needed to talk to me about remodeling his kitchen."

They both looked accusingly at Stavros, who was studiously ignoring their conversation. Yannis raised his voice. "So, Stavros, you want a new kitchen? I have the feeling your wife doesn't know anything about that."

"Well, uh…"

Cara joined in. "I'll be sure Athena tells her what a nice surprise you have for her. I bet you want the very best— cherry cabinets, granite countertops, marble floors."

"And don't forget the stainless-steel German appliances," Yannis added with a touch of maliciousness.

The bus driver hunched his wide shoulders over the steering wheel. "Yannis, *parakaló…*"

"Don't you 'please, Yannis' me, Stavros. What's the deal?"

Stavros looked up in the wide rearview mirror, his eyes pleading. "All right, all right. Athena wanted to surprise the two of you with a romantic bus ride into the heart of Aphrodisias." Just then Stavros hit a large pothole, sending them practically to the ceiling. The bus backfired, the smell of diesel fumes wafting through the window. Oh, yes, this was the essence of romance.

Yannis scoffed. "Give me a break, Stavros. You have to go along with every foolish notion an old lady tells you?"

It shouldn't have hurt Cara to hear he didn't want to spend time with her, since that was what she had intended by leaving tomorrow—but it did hurt.

"No, no, I swear. I didn't want to fool you like this, but Athena threatened to call my mother if I didn't help her." He wiped sweat off his forehead. "Please don't tell my wife about a new kitchen. She's begging me to remodel and I just can't afford it now. The bus needs a new exhaust system, fuel prices are terrible..." He ran out of breath.

Yannis looked at Cara, who shrugged. Despite their previous argument, she couldn't blame Stavros—he was a victim of meddling as much as they were. "Okay, okay." Yannis added in Greek, "We all know how women can be, right, *philos?*"

Cara rolled her eyes quickly, but Yannis caught her. "Hey, you understood that?"

"A bit. *Philos* is 'friend', right?"

"Yeah, not bad." Yannis slapped Stavros on the back. "See how smart this lady is, Stav? Only on the island a few weeks and picking up our language like *that*." He snapped his fingers.

Actually, Cara felt more dishonest than smart. "I studied a bit before I came, but you all speak so quickly, it's hard for a beginner to understand." It had taken Cara several months of Greek lessons with Athena before she could begin to understand native Greeks speaking with each other.

The men laughed, Stavros finally relaxing. Cara wished she could. There was still so much left unsaid between her and Yannis. Fortunately it would be a short bus tour and she could probably avoid a heavy-duty conversation where they were forced to hash out their differences. She'd raise a cloud of Greek dust running away from the bus once they returned to the village. "We Greeks just have a lot to say, right, Yannis? That's why we talk fast."

Yannis stared solemnly at her. "And we want to make sure everybody on the island can hear what we have to say, that's why we talk loud." He leaned over to Cara. "But some people never learn how to talk about things at all." Cara froze at his cold blue gaze. The bus pitched again and Cara stared straight ahead, trying to endure the bumpy, smelly ride somewhere into Back of Nowhere, Aphrodisias.

STAV NEEDED TO BUY new shocks as well as an exhaust system. About an hour later, which seemed like six to Yannis's severely bruised ass, Stav pulled over in a small clearing. Yannis stood up and frowned. "What are we doing here, Stav? There's nothing around but some rocks and weeds."

Stavros shrugged. "Don't ask me. I've never heard of this place and neither have the other tour-bus operators. But Athena says there's a grotto if you follow the trail for a half mile or so."

Cara furrowed her brow, obviously expecting some well-marked pathway. Yannis grimaced.

"See that worn spot in the grass? That's the trail," Stav told them. It disappeared behind some boulders and then reappeared several hundred yards up the hill.

"Nice day for a hike, eh?" Stavros gave him a wide, tour-bus operator grin. Too bad the only tip Yannis had for him was one that involved vulgar anatomical possibilities.

But Cara was already moving toward the door. "Oh, stay with Stavros if you don't feel like hiking, I won't be long. You have the whole summer to hike, after all."

He frowned. It sounded as if she didn't plan to hike anymore during the summer. Maybe she didn't want him around and was dumping him with Stav. Well, that was too bad, since they had unfinished business. But she was already down the steps. He followed, half considering telling Stav's wife about her fake new kitchen anyway. "You're not coming with us, are you, Stav?"

"No, no. You know my bad knee." He vaguely gestured at his pant leg. "Too much for me."

"Lay off the baklava, and you'll move around easier."

His friend glared at him, his mustache twitching in indignation. "Enjoy your hike, Yannis."

"Thanks a lot." He clattered out of the bus and followed Cara up the goat path. She had shouldered her backpack and walked ahead without acknowledging him. The path was too narrow to walk next to her, but at least he consoled himself with a great view. Not the island of course, but Cara. Her legs were creamy-golden and disappeared into khaki shorts that cupped her ass just the way he wanted to.

Maybe this hike wasn't quite a loss. She reached a gigantic boulder and turned to wait for him. "Oh, you're coming with me. I guess you want to talk about what happened—"

He shrugged nonchalantly, as if finding out she'd kept large parts of her life secret from him didn't bother him. "You don't want to talk, I don't talk."

"Oh." She was puzzled. "If you don't want to talk, what do you—"

He cut off her words with a hard kiss, spinning her out of sight of the bus and pressing her against the warm rock. She clutched his shoulders in surprise, but quickly melted in his arms, as she always had. At least that hadn't changed. He pulled back from her soft lips. "Tell me you still want this—you still want me."

She was fighting some internal battle—he could tell by her furrowed brow and set jaw. With a sigh, she pulled him back to her and whispered, "yes," into the hollow of his throat.

Yannis shoved down the sweeping sense of relief at her yielding to him and focused on making sure she'd never regret it. He slipped a hand under her tight white T-shirt and his other hand unzipped her shorts.

With another couple motions, her shorts and panties were around her ankles, her front-close bra flapped open and her T-shirt was around her neck. Her backpack cushioned her skin from the rock's surface, which would be good when he pushed inside her.

He was mindless as usual around Cara, focusing only on sucking on her pretty coral-tipped breasts and massaging her hard little clit. Her juices dampened his fingers and her face tightened as she gave short breathy cries, panting his name. He slid down her body and parted her plump folds to lick her sweet button, and her cries broadened into a scream.

She slumped forward onto him, and he gladly bore her weight. His awareness expanded to notice his rock-hard cock practically bulging out the leg of his shorts and he was about to figure out what do about it that didn't involve a nonexistent condom when he heard a familiar and ominous explosion.

"Shit!" Why was Stav firing up the bus? Yannis yanked Cara's shirt down and shorts up and charged down the hill to the clearing.

"What the hell!" A pile of luggage sat on the ground, and Stav was pulling away. "Stavros, get back here!" But the man only waved before tooting the horn nastily.

Yannis gave him an obscene gesture that merely earned him a faceful of Aphrodisian dust and a diminishing view of the blue-and-white bus. Coughing, he turned to the heap of suitcases.

Cara picked her way down the last meters to the clearing, her cheeks still pink and her eyes still glassy from her orgasm. "Yannis, where is Stavros going?"

He shrugged helplessly. "I have no idea. Wait—" He pulled a folded note off the top bag. Cara yanked it from his hand and opened the paper. "Oh, I don't believe this."

"What?" He craned his neck to read over her shoulder. She hadn't fixed her bra yet, so he could see the tips of her nipples under her shirt. Forcing himself to concentrate, he read the note written in English. "This is Athena's doing?"

Cara pursed her lips.

Dear Cara, as a treat to you and Yannis, I have arranged a romantic, rustic weekend at Aphrodite's Grotto. These supplies include everything you need to have a wonderful time together. Emma and Eleni helped pack for you, so they know you are gone. Stavros will come pick you up Sunday in plenty of time for Yannis's party. I am sure you both have plenty to talk about. All my love, Athena.

Cara shouted into the quiet air. "Athena, I'm going to strangle you!"

"What? Why would she strand us in the middle of nowhere?" And worst of all, without condoms, no doubt. Yannis unzipped one duffel bag and found clean clothes. Another had a small tent, and in two bags were sleeping bags. A cardboard box held camping rations and water. "Give me your cell phone, Cara. I'll call one of my cousins to come get us." The faster they got back to town, the faster he could take Cara to bed and make her forget she'd ever loved another man.

"Here." She handed it to him and he pressed several buttons.

"It's not turning on, and there should be service even out here." He slid open the battery compartment and showed her the empty slot.

"Great, somebody removed the battery. Try yours, then." Cara sucked her lower lip into her mouth, looking worried.

He shrugged helplessly. "Niko asked to borrow it and then forgot to give it back." Yannis would buy Niko a huge beer as soon as he saw him again. He fought back a grin, knowing Cara was genuinely concerned. As far as he was concerned, stranding him in the wilderness with a beautiful woman deserved a nice thank-you.

"Forgot on purpose, I bet."

Yannis walked around the clearing, stirring up the settling dust. "Looks like we're here until Stavros comes back for us Sunday, but where are we supposed to camp? Here in the road?" He didn't much care as long as they had the tent for privacy.

Cara showed him the paper. "Here's a map at the bottom of the note to the grotto she was talking about. I guess there's a pond or something there."

"Okay." Yannis eyed the pile and lifted the tent and duffel bag. "This'll take more than one trip. Grab what you can manage."

"What do we do with the rest of it?" Cara lifted a sleeping bag in each arm.

He balanced his load and started up the trail. "If somebody comes by to steal it while we're gone, they can offer us a ride back to town."

YANNIS TURNED A CORNER and gave a low whistle.

"What?" His broad shoulders blocked Cara's view. "What is it?"

"Come see." He moved to the side and Cara saw what had elicited his whistle. It wasn't a pond, as she'd thought from the map. It was an ancient hot spring about the size of an American backyard swimming pool, the opaque water the color of expensive pale green jade.

Three walls of a marble bathhouse stood at one end of the spring, a small arched opening in the back wall illuminating the spring's smooth, glassy surface. "I hope they packed swimsuits for us," Cara muttered, still shaky after her abrupt capitulation to Yannis's caresses. Despite her amazing sexual release, she was not thinking kindly of Emma and Athena's stunt, obviously designed to make her miss her ferry reservation. Probably Athena's cousins ran the reservation office, too.

"I don't," Yannis replied with a grin. "I've never heard of this hot spring. The popular ones are down on the coast near the hotels."

"A real hot spring." Cara set down the sleeping bags and

wondered if they zipped together into one big bag. "We may as well stay right here. The tent can go on the flat area over there."

"Okay." He dropped the tent gear where she pointed. "I'll go get the rest of the supplies and then put up the tent." He went back down the hill and she unzipped the tent bag.

Piece of cake. It was a modern backpacking tent and didn't require a second person for setup. Within a few minutes, she'd popped up the tent, rolled out mats for extra padding, and zipped together the sleeping bags after some consideration. It would be foolish to think she could be alone with Yannis all weekend and not want to touch his beautiful body or watch his handsome face tighten as she touched him.

Being out in the fresh air had mellowed her panicky mood somewhat, the trickling of the springwater in the grotto soothing her nerves. She carried the duffel into the tent to find out what Emma had packed for a "romantic, rustic weekend." Flannel and silk?

She laughed to find that wasn't far off the mark. Emma had tossed in several slinky nightgowns along with clean underwear and rolled-up hiking socks, pretty much what she had expected. But on top of the socks was a flowery-smelling paper bag.

Curious, she opened the bag and lifted out a note. Underneath was a pile of freshly picked pink rose petals. Rose petals to strew on a sleeping bag? That was taking it a bit far.

She unfolded the note.

Dear Cara, the petals are for an offering to the goddess Aphrodite. Toss them in her spring and wish for your heart's desire. Love, Athena.

Cara sat back on her heels. Now that was just silly. Rose petals in water might make a nice bath, but they would never grant her heart's desire. She shook her head and stuffed the note back into the paper bag. Rose petals aside, she hoped Athena had packed more toiletries than that to keep her smelling nice this weekend.

Yes, she'd even packed Cara's toiletry case, which bulged at the seams. Hoping it contained her deodorant and toothbrush, Cara unfastened the case and a mountain of condoms fell out on the sleeping bag.

A delighted whistle came from behind her. Cara shifted around to find Yannis rubbing his hands together. "I didn't think there were that many condoms on the island. Remind me to buy Emma a white wine when we get back to civilization."

Heat crawled up her face. "Maybe they're from Athena."

He grimaced. "I wouldn't be surprised, but at this point I don't care." He swept the packets off the sleeping bag save one, which he held up invitingly. "It would be rude to let these go to waste."

Cara just couldn't resist him—she knew that now. "We certainly don't want to be rude." She pulled her shirt and loose bra off in one swift motion, enjoying how his nostrils flared at the sight of her bare breasts. She shimmied out of her shorts and underwear and kicked off her hiking boots. "Wanna go for a swim?" She walked toward the water's edge, as she heard his clothing and work boots hit the ground.

"No, but how about some skinny-dipping?" He swept her up against his own naked body and tested the water with his toe. "Perfect." He carried her into the spring, the warm water lapping around her bottom. He stopped and slowly sank them both until they were shoulder-deep, sitting side by side on a built-in marble bench below the surface.

Cara sighed and closed her eyes, the heat relaxing muscles she didn't realize were tight. It was like being in a hot bath, but more slippery and buoyant from the mineral content. She rolled her shoulders and neck. "Oh, that's lovely."

"Yes, you are."

She looked at him in surprise, his blue gaze intent on her face.

"Always, to me." Yannis continued, "When I kiss you here." He kissed her lips gently. "And here." He gave her little kisses over her cheeks. "And here." He kissed the column of her neck. "And when I touch you here."

She felt the ripples of his hand moving through the water and then he cupped her. "Your plump breast filling my hand, reacting as I play with you."

Cara swung her leg over his lap to fully face him. He quickly found the juncture of her thighs. "And here—the sweet place I need to be." He pulled her hand down to his cock and to her surprise, he was already wearing a condom. He must have put it on when he undressed. "Let me come in you, sweet Cara."

Her answer was a sweet kiss on his lips. He caught her around the hips and eased into her. They both sighed as he sank deep, reaching her inner core he had just barely teased behind the boulder a half hour ago.

"Yes, Yannis." Using the bench for leverage, Cara rose and lowered herself onto him. Her movements were slow and purposeful as the warm water ebbed and flowed where they were joined. She took the time to smooth back a stray glossy curl from his brow. To kiss his forehead, and to draw patterns in the black hair that cushioned his gold medallion—Agios Ioannis Prodromos, of course, St. John the Baptist, whose feast day she would celebrate after all, before leaving Aphrodisias.

She shook her head.

"What, Cara *mou?*" His glazed-over eyes hadn't missed her hesitation.

"Nothing." She moved faster on him, determined to make their time in the spring a memorable one. Religion was quickly forgotten and the sheer pagan nature of the place took over. Yannis dug his fingers into her butt and thrust up into her.

His lips captured her wet nipple as it bobbed out of the water, his hard suction washing down to her clit. He let go of her for a second, and she frowned down at him.

He grinned up at her. "Mmm, salty. Like some other places I like to lick." He stroked her tiny knot of nerves between them and Cara felt herself swell into his touch. She yanked his head to her breasts, muffling his self-satisfied chuckle.

His stubble skidded over her wet flesh and she dug her fingers into his slippery shoulders at the sweet friction. The merciless water caressed every inch of her outer being while his cock glided deep inside her. Her emotions were not neglected, either, thanks to the sweet things he was murmuring to her in Greek, half of which she missed because of the growing roar in her ears.

Suddenly her orgasm rushed over her like a dammed river breaking its banks. "Oh, Yannis, Yannis," she cried, the turbulent water washing over where his cock pleasured her.

"Cara, Cara *mou,* lovely Cara," he chanted, diving into her again. His beautiful face, so much like a classical statue, took on an expression that was all man as he groaned his pleasure at being inside her.

The water gradually calmed around them, and Yannis raised his lips for a kiss. "Ah, Cara, what you do to me."

"And you, too, Yannis." So they nestled still joined while the sun shone through the arched window and cast flickering patterns on the jade-colored water.

12

CARA COLLAPSED next to Yannis on a blanket at the edge of the spring. "Oh, Yannis, that was wonderful." Yannis had spent a long night in the cozy tent pleasuring her and they had stoked up with a Saturday-morning breakfast of protein bars before running back to the spring. Their quick cleanup had turned into a slow, sensual exploration half-in, half-out of the spring. She was his water nymph, his insatiable muse.

"Well, Cara, you make me crazy for you." Yannis shoved his hand through his wild tangle of curls. He really needed to find a comb, but didn't care a bit at this point. Cara leaned over and kissed his forehead.

"Is that a bad thing?" she asked coyly, running her hand down his belly.

"I am a satyr around you. You look at me and I harden." He gestured down to his erection, which never seemed to go away when he touched her. Or was near her. Or even thought of her.

"A satyr? I saw one of those painted on a vase in Athens. He actually had a wineglass balanced on his erection." Cara reached for a water bottle and pretended to set it on top of him.

He sat up in protest, automatically raising his hand in self-protection. "Hey!"

"All right, all right." Cara giggled and set the bottle down. He snuggled her onto his shoulder and stroked her silky back. They were under a small tree that wouldn't afford them much shade soon once the sun was overhead. He needed to rub some sunscreen onto the pale triangles usually covered by her bikini. She had loved it before when he massaged her breasts with the slick lotion....

"And what do you think your aunt and uncle will say about you disappearing for the weekend?"

Okay, now his erection was subsiding. "I am a man. I answer to no one but myself." He winked at her to let her know he was joking. She seemed touchy about the macho aspects of Greek culture.

"And I am a woman. I answer to no one but myself." She gave him a haughty look.

"Except Athena." He kissed her shoulder.

She made a growling noise. "She's gone too far this time."

"Okay, *not* Athena." He laughed but then grew serious. "I have an idea. Just for now, why don't we answer to each other?"

"EACH OTHER?" Cara wasn't sure what he meant. Answer to each other? She gave him a puzzled look and then realization dawned and she bit her lip. She'd gone from self-reliance as a single woman to utter dependence on her husband and then back to a shaky sense of independence. Yannis's suggestion was something new.

"Yeah, each other." He gave her a quick smile. "I look out for you, and you look out for me. These hills are pretty wild—you never know what could come roaring out of them—minotaurs, centaurs, cyclopses—"

"Goats, donkeys, rabbits," she interrupted, trying to avoid his real question.

It didn't work. "So what do you say, Cara *mou?* Will you protect me from the wild bunnies?"

"Okay, Yannis. And will you protect me from…" She was about to say "myself," but knew that wasn't true anymore. The only danger she posed to herself was letting her heart get broken.

He was waiting for her to finish her sentence, so she tried again. "Will you protect me from any feral goats?"

"Absolutely." He kissed her, but not before she saw a flash of disappointment in his eyes at her hesitation. She hated to be the one who put it there, but she didn't know what else to say.

She sighed as his breathing slowed. It was simple for him. He got up every day, went to work and came home to his doting aunt. Replace his aunt with a wife in a few years and his life would continue on, probably much like his uncle's—tied into the island's rhythms and cycles, adjusting to the times, but remaining essentially the same.

A rose-scented breeze wafted to her. Those rose petals again. Yannis had mentioned the scent in her luggage last night, but she'd told him it came from a potpourri sachet. He'd nodded uncomprehendingly, obviously writing it off as some girlie thing.

Her heart's desire. No, she wouldn't wish for something like that when she wasn't even sure what it was. Yannis shifted under her, his big, warm hand coming up to rest on her shoulder. Cara buried her face in his neck, inhaling his salty male scent, the firm muscles of his chest cushioning her breasts. Even in sleep he was sexy, his penis still half-hard from their lovemaking.

Oh, who was she kidding? *Yannis* was her heart's desire. It would be crazy to wish for him, knowing what a jinx she would be for him or any man.

But the beautiful grotto smelled like a rose garden in full bloom, stronger and stronger until she had to see just what kind of rose petals Athena had packed.

She slipped reluctantly from Yannis's embrace and tiptoed to the tent. The paper bag still sat in her duffel. She couldn't smell the petals until she opened the bag, and they were wilting and turning brown around the edges in the summer heat.

It wouldn't hurt to throw them in the spring. At least she and Yannis might have a colorful swim. She scurried back to the pool.

Boy, that rose smell was everywhere. Maybe there was a wild thicket of roses over the hill. She opened the bag and tossed the few handfuls of petals onto the water, their bruised and fading surfaces contrasting sadly with the vibrant green water.

Just then, Yannis murmured in Greek, "Cara, come back to me."

Embarrassed, she spun around and his sleepy smile undid her heart. *Oh, I wish this could never end.* The thought popped into her head before she could help it.

So be it. She'd wished for lots of things that had never come to pass, and a few sickly rose petals wouldn't change that losing streak.

Yannis must have dozed a bit, thanks to his long night, since the sun was at a higher angle when he opened his eyes again. Cara slept tucked into his chest, but he could see the pinkness starting on her skin. He wasn't exactly accustomed to nude sunbathing, either, and wasn't eager to find out if certain areas burned or not. "Cara, wake up. You need some sun lotion."

"What?" She tipped her face up to him, her eyes heavy

with sleep. Her tongue came out to moisten her plump lips and he groaned. She gave him a knowing smile and leaned over to run her tongue over his mouth. He opened eagerly and let her nibble and suck at his lips, finding her nipple with his fingers and playing with it until it swelled and peaked under his fingers.

He went to roll her under him, but she stopped him. "Wait, Yannis. I want to please you." She pushed him onto his back and moved over his thighs. Her breasts swayed tantalizingly, their coral tips darkening with arousal as she reached for the water bottle.

He was hard enough to support the bottle by now, but fortunately she didn't try that. "Lie back. I'll clean you." He hesitated, but wanted to see what she had in mind. She grabbed a clean towel from their interrupted bath and poured some water on it. He hissed in shock as she dabbed his shaft and head, wiping every inch with the cool cloth. She moved down to his balls, cupping and lifting them until they tightened dangerously.

He moaned and called out her name, grabbing at her breasts, her ass, her clit, wherever he could reach. He was so crazed with lust he was about to lift her and plant her on top of his bare cock, protection or no.

She must have been aware how close he was to the edge since she moved back from him. "And now for a rinse." Her voice was unsteady, but her movements weren't as she squeezed the cloth over him, the water soaking his entire groin and running down into the blanket under him. He'd never felt anything like that before, and his cock agreed, turning purple in the sunlight.

"Nice and clean." Cara tugged at his hands until he struggled to his feet, guiding him over to the pool.

"Cara, what are all these flowers?"

She turned to see what he saw and she gasped.

The water's surface was entirely covered in rose petals—red, white and every shade of pink.

"I, um, tossed a few into the water—you know, for a romantic effect," Cara explained.

"It's very romantic." He wondered briefly how on earth Athena had packed several pounds of petals without him noticing them, but then their sultry scent buzzed through his brain. "Are we going for a swim?"

Cara blinked and turned to him, her blue eyes hazy with desire. "No, I am." She tugged him down to sit on the marble tile surrounding the spring, his feet dangling into the hot, flowery water.

Then she did the unexpected and slipped into the spring, gliding to face him.

Her red curls floated behind her, her breasts peeping out of their floral blanket. He couldn't see her lower body, and for a crazy minute, she was a real water nymph emerging from her spring to ease his poor mortal pain.

But then she opened her hot, sweet mouth to enfold him and his pain spiked into agony. She sucked at him as if he were wild honey, his foreskin slipping back and forth under her tongue as she reached the exquisitely sensitive tip underneath. He clenched the side of the pool until his fingertips went numb.

Her motions were slow and leisurely due to the water, and for one horrible second, she even stopped. He thrust into her mouth and groaned. Her rosy lips widened into a smug smile around him.

"Cara!" He wrapped his hands in her hair, trapping her in the juncture of his thighs. "*Parakaló*, Cara *mou, glykha mou, thea mou...*" He was calling her his sweet, his goddess, all the fine and good things she was. She sped up at his plea, her slippery fingers tickling and pressing his balls, cold against the marble.

Her eyes were closed and she made little hums of satisfaction, buzzing his cock until he thought he'd scream. He was dizzy with lust, drunk with desire, drugged with lechery, as if he were that satyr at an orgy. But the only one he wanted was Cara. He looked down at her beautiful face and rich hair and couldn't last a second longer.

His climax exploded through him, drawing up from his toes to his cock and pouring into her magical, mystical mouth. He spasmed over her and his feelings flooded out of him, as well. "Oh, Cara, *eime erotevmenos mazi sou, eime erotevmenos mazi sou,* Cara." He loved her—he loved her. It had hit him with all the force of his orgasm—he *did* love her, crazily, passionately, tenderly. He'd loved her ever since he'd found her crying in her sleep from that headache.

She pulled back from him, her eyes wide at his outburst. Thankfully she didn't understand much Greek, or else she'd totally freak out. He hadn't planned to fall in love with her, but how could he not? She was perfect for him— smart, beautiful, funny. He decided not to tell her in English yet, so he gave her a bland look and slipped under the water next to her. "Hey, you. Come here."

She was still looking at him warily as he tugged her close. "What were you telling me, Yannis?"

"Well, *'glykha mou'* is 'my sweet' and *'thea mou'* is 'my goddess'. That's all."

"Oh." Cara relaxed at his casual approach and went into his embrace. That wasn't all, but it was enough for now.

YANNIS KISSED CARA'S FOREHEAD, his lips warm and sweet on her skin. Her limbs were heavy and relaxed from the spring, and she floated in his strong, brown arms for several minutes. With her cheek resting on his chest, she listened to the gradually quieting thump of his heart. It still amazed her that she had such an effect on such a sexy man as Yannis, but his response to her was unmistakable.

But Yannis couldn't *possibly* love her. It had only been a couple weeks since they met, and her own husband hadn't loved her even after several years. She sighed in self-pity and then frowned at herself.

"Tired?" He had mistaken her sigh for a yawn.

"What?" She looked up into his heavy-lidded blue eyes. "Maybe a little. We *were* up most of the night."

"I'll take you to bed for a nap."

Cara yelped in surprise as he wrapped his big hands around her waist and lifted her out of the spring to set her on the cool marble edge where he'd just sat. Her nipples tightened as the breeze skimmed her skin.

Yannis noticed, too, leaning forward to capture one in his mouth. She yelped again, this time in delight, as he sucked her deep, flicking her with his tongue. She threaded her fingers through his slick, dark curls, water beading up on his smooth back like diamonds in the morning sun. "Oh, Yannis," she whimpered. He was an assault on the careful walls she had built around her, cracking them gradually every time they made love.

He looked up at her with his devilish grin and let go of her nipple. "You'll like this even better." He slid his open mouth down her belly. She cried out as he unerringly found her clit with his tongue, darting and licking the slick nub. He moved his mouth over her lush, damp folds and rubbed his stubbled cheeks slowly over her tender skin, despite her attempts to urge him on.

He started murmuring in Greek as he stroked her clit

with his fingers. "So sweet, so hot, I die for the taste of you, the scent of you, finer than wine…" His sexy words faded into appreciative groans as he dived back onto her with his mouth. Cara loved hearing the secret things he spoke to her, and she swelled under his tongue, spikes of sensation reaching deep into her pussy. She grabbed his slick shoulders in a futile attempt to drag him out of the water and into her, but he easily resisted her efforts. "No, no, Cara, let me please you."

Oh, he did please her, especially when he licked her with long, strong strokes reaching deep inside her. She squirmed and wiggled on the marble trying to ease her ache. He knew exactly what she needed before she knew, sliding first one finger and then a second where his tongue had just darted into her.

She immediately shuddered around him, and he stopped licking her clit long enough to give her a satisfied grin. "More?"

She shook her head. "Too much, too much."

"Not with me." He returned to his task, this time gently wiggling his fingers back and forth until he hit a magic spot she hadn't known existed until he'd found it. His lips captured her clit in delicate suction and the terrible, delicious tension spiraled throughout her.

She stared down at him in dazed fascination, his black head brushing her red curls, his sun-darkened hands gripping and spreading her pale thighs wide to receive him.

She was a marble goddess worshipped by her mortal lover, a stone object gradually coming to life under his ministrations. Her fair skin flushed from her belly up to her breasts, her nipples darkening and jutting even more. She cupped her breasts and tentatively brushed her thumbs over their tips. It felt so good that she pinched herself. A hedonistic cry escaped her lips. How had she never experienced this before?

Startled, Yannis looked up at her, his perfectly shaped mouth dripping with her juices. She fisted her hand in his curls and dragged him up to her by his hair. She wanted to experience everything in their wild place of love and crushed her mouth to his.

She could smell and taste herself on his firm lips, but it was arousing, not distasteful, to have the same sensations on her mouth as on her clit. To know that he had created this response in her and they both fully enjoyed it. His hot skin slipped over hers, her nipples catching in his chest hair. He worked his fingers inside her again and she suddenly needed his attention back there.

She shoved his head back between her thighs and fondled her breasts again. She thought she heard a muffled chuckle, but was too close to coming to notice much but his and her touch in union. Locking her ankles around his neck, she rocked back and forth against his sucking, lapping touch. When he scraped her clit with his teeth and the last bits of her stony facade cracked away, her passion for him burst free as she writhed under his mouth and hands. "Oh, Yannis, Yannis…" She trailed off into a wordless cry. Sweet shards of desire pierced her whole body and she shook in his embrace.

After an eternity of pleasure so intense it bordered on pain, she pressed a kiss to his head. He tipped up his face to hers. "Thank you, Cara *mou.*"

"For what?" She should be thanking him for how she felt.

He lifted her around the waist and helped her slide into the soothing water of the spring. "For being here with me. I've never enjoyed anything like our time together." He nuzzled her hair.

"Thank you, Yannis." His sincerity and honesty touched her, yet saddened her at the same time. He deserved somebody equally sincere and honest, and once she left, he'd find somebody much better than she.

13

YANNIS SET the last of Cara's camping luggage in her living room. Cara dropped her backpack on the couch and stretched her aching spine. "Oh, that feels good. The bus ride back from the grotto wasn't any smoother than the ride there."

"Don't do that unless you want me to stay." His gleaming gaze was fastened on how her breasts jutted out when she arched her back.

She giggled. "Haven't you had enough, Yannis?"

"Of you? Never." He caught her around the waist and nuzzled her neck.

That sounded suspiciously romantic, so she edged out of his embrace just as Emma came out of her bedroom. "Hey, I thought I heard voices. How was your trip?"

"Into the back of beyond? Where my cell phone battery was mysteriously missing?" Cara tried to sound censorious, but failed.

"I'll let the two of you catch up." Yannis tipped up her chin and kissed her lips. "I'll see you tonight at the party, Cara."

"Okay," Cara replied. She couldn't resist seeing him again as soon as possible.

"Emma, you did a great job packing." He winked at them both and headed out.

Emma turned to Cara. "What did he mean, I did a great job packing?"

Cara's face heated. "All those condoms, probably. Where on earth did you get so many? There had to be at least twenty."

Her friend's eyes widened. "I only had two to put in there. Athena must have…ewww." They both groaned and Cara flopped down on the orange couch.

"Em, I really should chew you out for going along with her plotting, but that woman's a force of nature."

Emma collapsed next to her. "Like the volcano that destroyed Santorini. Or the earthquake they think sank Atlantis."

"Only more troublesome." They looked at each other and laughed.

"Come on, Cara, didn't you have a nice time up there? Athena said you and Yannis needed to be alone."

"That place was about as alone as you can get," Cara allowed. "But yes, we camped next to an ancient hot spring, swam, slept, talked…" Talked, but not about the biggest thing he'd let slip, not knowing she understood his every word of love.

Emma patted her hand. "It sounds fabulous. I wish Nick and I could have more time alone, but his mother always worries if he stays out too much."

Cara nodded, but didn't believe that was his mother's motive. As if Nick's mother didn't know exactly where he was, on such a small and close-knit island? Ha.

Yannis had said his parents wouldn't be at his party, since they couldn't leave London because his sister had just had a baby. Not that she wanted to meet his parents or have him meet hers—she still planned to leave Greece as soon as the next ferry docked. He was a nice guy and didn't deserve the trouble she could inadvertently cause him.

And if Yannis *did* think he was falling in love with her, her sudden departure would cure him of that.

She reached up to push a curl off her forehead and grimaced. "Ugh. The hot spring was great, but the water was full of minerals. I think my hair is calcified by now."

Emma jumped up and extended a hand to help her off the couch. "Hop in the shower. The party doesn't start until after dark, so there's plenty of time for you to even take a nap." Emma stood back and crossed her arms over her chest. "Hmm, you do look pretty tired. Did the crickets keep you awake all night?" she teased.

"Something kept me up all night, but it was bigger than a cricket," she joked back.

"You know, Cara, I think the Aphrodisias effect has done you a world of good. Before we came, you were quiet and wore black all the time. Now you're laughing, wearing bright colors, enjoying yourself."

Emma was too polite to mention Cara's torrid summer affair, but they both knew what she meant. "Are you having a good summer, too, Emma?"

Emma hugged her enthusiastically. "Oh, yes, Cara, thank you. I never would have been able to stay on Aphrodisias for the whole summer if you hadn't treated me. I would have missed all of this—the beautiful island, the beach, Nick…" She finished with a blush.

Cara almost changed her mind about leaving. She knew Emma's conscience wouldn't let her stay if Cara left, even if Cara paid for the rest of the summer's stay. Maybe Cara could lie low in Crete for a week or so to try to put her head together.

"And you never would have met Yannis." Emma smiled at her. "I think he's falling in love with you."

"You do?" Cara's insides chilled. "Why do you think that?"

Her friend shrugged. "Just women's intuition. Don't you think so?"

"No." Cara turned on stiff legs and headed to the bathroom. Yannis hated liars, he'd said so himself. And while she'd told him the partial truth about Con, she still hadn't fully opened up to him. "He doesn't know me well enough to love me," she called to Emma. And if he *did* know her better, he would never love her.

CARA PARKED Athena's compact car in front of Yannis's aunt and uncle's house. She'd never been there before, but judging from the four hundred or so people milling around, she figured she was at the right place. They lived a short distance from town in a typically cubic, whitewashed house. Lights blazed from all the rectangular windows, and Greek pop music blared from jumbo speakers set up in the yard.

Athena had assured her that the excavation was in the hands of the government now, and Uncle Gus had thrown up his hands in typically Greek fatalism at the delay of his deal. Athena had extended him the proverbial olive branch and connected him with another of her relatives who had a nice parcel of land for sale, so everyone was happy.

"This looks like a pretty fancy party. Are you sure we don't need to bring any birthday presents for Yannis?" Emma looked at the small box of pastries from the local bakery.

Cara shook her head. "It's not his birthday, and Athena says around here people just bring some sweets or wine for a name day party." She lifted a bottle of local ouzo. "We've got both covered."

"I suppose you can always give him an extra-special present later. I asked Athena if I could sleep at her house tonight. You know, just to give you guys a little more privacy."

"Oh, Emma, you don't have to do that—"

Emma held up her hand. "Really, it's not a big deal. I tossed an overnight case into the back of the car. Athena will give me a ride back to her place and you and Yannis can hang off the chandelier for all I care."

Cara laughed and shook her head. Emma had done her own share of blossoming during their trip. While Cara had her doubts about Niko's motives, he seemed to be helping Emma lighten up and enjoy herself after years of study. "Come on, let's go find the guys."

They walked up the yard past men poking at half a dozen sides of lamb and kabobs the size of fencing rapiers over a flaming fire pit. The men looked up and stared at Cara and Emma in the typically blunt but not rudely sexual manner of Greek men. Cara barely noticed it anymore, but Emma twitched uneasily at being the center of attention.

"We just walk in?" Emma asked as they approached the wide-open front door.

"Who's going to hear the doorbell if we ring it?" Cara pointed out as she entered. "The women are in the kitchen, so we'll take the food there."

A burst of high-pitched laughter guided them to the kitchen at the back of the house.

The laughter stopped as soon as Cara and Emma entered, mostly teenage girls and young women sitting around. The Greek women wore their most fashionable clothes and frequently shook out long, straight layers of dark hair. Cara looked good tonight, too, her square-necked sundress the color of ripe cantaloupe, its straps crisscrossing a mostly bare back. She'd even bothered to straighten her hair for the first time in a long time.

"Hello," Emma said awkwardly. "Has anyone seen Yannis?"

"Which one? There are eleven here," one of the teen-agers answered, her friends snickering. One particularly snotty-looking girl made a crack in Greek about stupid, fat American women.

The "stupid" crack bugged Cara the most. She turned and gave the mouthy one a hard glance. "Yannis with the blue eyes. *My* boyfriend," she answered in perfect Greek, publicly calling him what he really was. Her first boyfriend in ages, but much more. "Isn't he handsome?"

The women looked at her in surprise, but most of them nodded in agreement. One petite brunette announced, "If he weren't my cousin, I'd go to bed with him in a second!"

"That never stopped you before, Angelika!" her friend catcalled among a chorus of hooting. Emma looked ques-tioningly at Cara. Cara gave her what she hoped was a re-assuring glance.

Emma looked over Cara's shoulder. "Oh, see, here's Yannis," she said in relief.

Cara spun around. Yannis stood at the back door, a curl tumbling down his forehead, his smile widening as he took in her appearance. He moved quickly toward her and pulled her into a deep kiss in front of everybody.

She was embarrassed to be the center of attention, but the magic of his embrace immediately blocked out every-thing else.

He finally pulled away from her. Ignoring the whispers and giggles, he stared at her. "You straightened your hair." Yannis stroked it as if he'd never touched it before. "It's so soft and smooth. And long." His eyes heated, and she knew he wanted to incorporate her temporary look into some bedroom games.

"I had some extra time to blow-dry it and, well, I wanted to take a nap and I knew sleeping on wet, curly hair was a bad idea."

He threw back his head and laughed. "You're so honest, Cara." She flinched, but he didn't notice. "Come on and meet my aunt Eleni. Theia Eleni! Meet Cara—she's my American girl I told you about."

Aunt Eleni came out from the pantry with a platter of stuffed grape leaves. She was short and plump with elaborately teased black hair and heavy makeup. "What, Yannis?" Her smile faded as she saw him with his arm around Cara's shoulder. His aunt obviously knew of Cara's connection to Athena and her roadblocks to the construction company. Despite Gus's pleasure with his new building site, Eleni held a grudge. That was okay. Cara was protective of Yannis, as well, although he'd never understand why.

After introducing them, Yannis steered her out into the backyard. More barbecues were flaming along, the men drinking and poking at the meat, tiki torches shining off their beer bottles. Yannis greeted them cheerfully, but didn't stop to talk. "I want to show you something." He stopped on the far side of a big equipment shed.

"What? Your tools?"

"One of them, if you're a good girl." He kissed her hard and long, his lips and tongue making her forget half the island was fifty feet away.

He couldn't stop touching her hair. "You look blond in this torch light—almost like another person."

"Blond?" She patted her hair nervously. She hadn't worn straight, blond hair since Con died, partly to take back her real self and partly to confuse people about her former identity.

"Don't worry, I like your hair the way it truly is." He leaned closer to whisper. "All those red ringlets to sink my fingers into as I sink into your body." He sucked her ear-lobe and she shut her eyes at the hot, wet sensation.

He palmed her breast through her dress and her eyes flew open. "No, Yannis, you can't. Most of your family is right around the corner."

"Doesn't a man deserve a special treat on his name day?" He leisurely found her nipple and teased it into a hard peak. "It would be a treat for you, too."

It sure would, Cara knew. Every time they had sex, it just got better, deeper and emotionally intimate on a level she'd never experienced before. As if making love with Yannis was her refuge. But she caught his stroking hand and pushed it away just the same. "Your special treat will have to wait until there aren't three hundred people within a hundred yards. Now let's try some of those lamb kabobs. I haven't eaten grilled lamb in years."

"Okay, okay." He relented good-naturedly. "Food first, then our other appetites later."

Cara let him guide her back to the party, their fingers entwined as if they were a real couple. She fought back nerves. If it took such self-control just to remove his hand from her breast at a busy party, how could she ever bring herself to leave him?

"MORE *TORTA?* Or *elliniko?*" Eleni hovered over Cara, offering her more cake and coffee as several women sat outside in the garden after the main meal was consumed. Yannis was off with the men, where there was raucous laughter and a lot of clinking of shot glasses likely filled with ouzo or retsina. With a small smile she realized she trusted him enough to know she wouldn't feature in any stories.

Thanks to Eleni's searching looks, Cara was antsy and didn't need any more caffeine. *"Oxi, efkhareestó."* Rats, she'd slipped back into Greek when she'd said "no, thank you" to the food.

Eleni nodded and went back to whisper to her friends. Cara looked for Athena, but the older lady was sitting with her friends in the living room. Cara sipped at her bottled water, wondering who to chat with. The younger girls only spoke Greek, and it was way too late for Cara to reveal her language skills. She sighed and stared over the torch-lit garden as a Greek dance mix played in the background. It was the same song that had played at the disco the first night she had met Yannis—the pop paean to summer sluttiness. Especially if you were a foreign girl wearing a tiny bikini and prone to spring-break-type public drunkenness according to the music video she'd seen on Greek TV last week.

The younger girls giggled at some of the risqué lyrics as Eleni and her friends frowned in disapproval, casting sidelong glances at Cara. Was it possible they recognized her? Would they pump Yannis for details and possibly give her away? She set down her water and went looking for Emma.

Emma was coming out of the bathroom, her cheeks and lips flushed pink.

"What's up, Em?"

Emma grabbed her hand and dragged her to a relatively quiet corner outside the front door. "Nick just left to visit his uncle Ianni's own name day party. But before he went, we had a *talk*."

"What did you *talk* about?" she asked, laying the same significant emphasis on the verb.

"Us." Emma was practically giddy with excitement.

"And the two of you are…?"

Emma took a deep breath. "I'm taking some time off school to stay here on Aphrodisias with Nick."

Cara narrowed her eyes. "How much time?"

Emma looked cagey. "I don't know. Maybe a semester, or two. Or a couple years."

Cara's jaw dropped. Emma was less than a year away from earning her Ph.D. from one of the best universities in the world. "Are you crazy, Emma? You're going to throw away your whole academic career for some guy? What are you going to do with a half-finished grad degree in theoretical mathematics on this tiny island? Bookkeeping? You don't even balance your checkbook half the time."

"Nick makes a good living, and we're talking about getting married." Emma stuck her chin out. "Until then, we could live with his family."

"You haven't even *met* his family!" And she knew what they thought of Emma, if they thought of her at all. Cara shoved her hands into her apparently blond, straight hair and tried to keep from pulling out large chunks.

"Don't do it, Emma. You don't know how these people think. His mother will hate your guts and his family will never accept you."

Her stubborn friend shook her head. "They'll come around."

"Emma, this isn't *My Big, Fat Greek Wedding.* They don't want you. You're smarter than all of them put together and here's the big point in neon lights—you are *not* Greek." Cara knew she was starting to lose it, but couldn't help herself, blood roaring in her ears. "Even if Niko somehow grew a pair and married you against their wishes, he would never stick up for you. Greek men are like that. Just look at me—do you think my loving Greek husband ever took my side? Hell, no! His family called me the vilest names possible while Con fucked around on me and nobody ever said boo."

"Cara, it's not the same." Emma extended a calming hand, but had a frightened expression. "Cara…"

"What? Don't you want to know what it's like to marry a Greek man?" She was shaking by then.

"Your husband was a Greek man?" Yannis had come around the house from the backyard.

Cara immediately spotted his blue eyes wide with shock. "I was foolish enough to fall in love with him, or rather who I thought he was."

Just then Yannis's Aunt Eleni barreled out of the house, Athena close on her heels and yelling her head off. "It's true, it's true!" Eleni yelped in Greek. "This girl, she is Karoleena. It's the hair—blond, straight hair!"

"Shut up, Eleni!" Athena shook her fist at Yannis's aunt, but Cara shook her head.

"What girl is Karoleena?" Yannis looked puzzled.

"Oh, I forgot, you were at the university in Ohio during her great scandal and didn't see the photos. They were all over the magazines and television."

"The university in Ohio?" Cara turned to him. "You went to school in Ohio?"

"He still does," Eleni continued. "Top of his class in architecture."

"You're speaking Greek. Very well." He gave Cara a narrow glance.

"And you're a university student less than two hundred miles from me?" At least Cara hadn't been the only close-mouthed one.

"She ought to speak Greek well. I spent years teaching her," Athena bragged. "Karoleena can speak, read and write almost like a native."

Cara grimaced. Bad timing.

"You understood everything I said to you." He was obviously remembering how he'd told her he'd loved her, but in Greek only.

She went to Yannis. "Remember the American blond trophy wife who had the 'good luck' to have her husband die while he bounced around on his mistress? The one who took half his money and went back to the States a wealthy woman?" She spread her arms wide. "Here I am. Heavier, healthier and definitely not a blonde."

Yannis stared at her as if she'd socked him in the gut.

"You see? You see?" his aunt shrilled. "She used her poor, dead husband's money to ruin your uncle's construction project. All for some stupid women's museum."

Athena started shouting at the woman in Cara's defense. Yannis ignored them and spoke to her. "Is it true? You are Karoleena Constantinos?"

"I used to be. After Con died, I took back my own name. And my own life."

He seemed too shocked to take it in. "I don't believe this. After all you and I... You couldn't even do me the courtesy to tell me your whole story. No, it is bits and parts and half-truths until the only way I learn about you is from other people." He shook his head. "Why couldn't you tell me?"

"Yannis, you don't understand. If people had known I was here it would have wrecked everything. I couldn't let anything wreck you, too."

"I am not some weak little boy to be wrecked, Karoleena." His face hardened until he appeared much older. "I am a man—but obviously you do not think so."

Before she could stop him, he hopped on his scooter and gunned the engine, driving into the night.

"Yannis!" She ran after him and looked back at Athena

for advice, as always. But Athena was lost in the crowd, fascinated and drawn by the noise and spectacle.

But Athena didn't hold answers for Cara—Cara would need to find them on her own. She had leaned on the older woman for years in order to survive in her gilded cage.

Con had built her gilded cage, but Cara had walked in and locked the door of her own accord. She could have left him when she discovered his fifteen-year affair, could have avoided falling into bulimia, could have confided in Athena and her family and gotten help. It was time to stop blaming her own disasters on other people and fix her own damn life.

What did she want with her life?

Yannis. Just as she'd wished at Aphrodite's grotto while tossing those petals. She loved Yannis, shaking in the dark with that monumental self-discovery. She wanted him in her life. Not to be her whole life, since she'd learned that painful lesson, but to weave him into her existence.

Despite his youth, he was a real man, not a boy. She should have told him everything and not tried to put him in his own gilded cage, an unwitting toy for her to take out and play with on her vacation.

She'd existed in a drab world of gray skies and black clothing until coming to Aphrodisias, and it was as if she were Dorothy stepping from Kansas into the Land of Oz. Magic happened here, too—hadn't she seen for herself how a handful of dried roses had bloomed over a whole pool? Talk about stopping to smell the roses. She was ready for love, ready to live her life again, ready for a loving life with Yannis.

But she couldn't explain all of that to him if she couldn't find him. Ignoring the stares and pointed fingers starting to aim in her direction, Cara ran to where the scooters were parked and picked one that didn't need keys.

Jabbing the push-button ignition, she swung her leg over the seat when the engine turned over. A cry went up from someone in the crowd, probably the scooter's owner, but Cara roared into the street and away from the party.

"Whoa!" The scooter wobbled a bit underneath her and she forced herself to concentrate on driving for a minute. It had been years since she'd driven a scooter, but it quickly came back to her.

Now, with the motorbike under control, she needed to find Yannis. It was only a short distance to the beach where they'd first frolicked in the ocean. She pulled into the parking lot, but it was empty. He probably needed more time to cool off, if he even stopped anywhere. She thought for a second. She didn't know all his haunts around the island, but one came to mind. She gunned the engine and hoped she could find it in the dark.

"SON OF A BITCH!" Yannis punched the old olive tree's trunk and then immediately wished he hadn't. His knuckles were no match for something that had withstood two thousand years. He paced around the tree, blowing on his lacerated skin.

The pain was slight compared to his heart. Stupid, stupid Yannis. Looking back, there were all sorts of clues that Cara had been keeping secrets from him. How she had learned Greek so quickly. How she was supposedly a college student but had plenty of money for what even he could tell were nice clothes and jewelry in addition to a whole summer's stay on an expensive Greek island. How Athena treated her like a second daughter but was unusually closemouthed about Cara's past when she gossiped about everyone else.

"*Gamoto!*" He let loose with a blistering string of

Greek curses, mostly aimed at himself. What a fool he was. What an utter fool to fall under her spell like a sailor lured onto the rocks by a Siren. Lured by her radiant smile, her sun-red hair and her luxuriant body, but bound by what he thought was her growing affection for him—or even love.

Just like that first night after the discotheque, he was her lovesick pet goat led around on a string. He howled his pain and rage up at the merciless full moon, just another witness to his stupidity and foolishness.

CARA SLOWED the scooter as she crested the hill leading to the old olive tree. At first she didn't see anyone there, but a dark figure separated from the black, shadowy trunk.

"Cara?" Yannis shaded his eyes as her headlight illuminated him.

"Hello, Yannis." She came to a stop and gingerly got off the scooter. "I'm sorry I ruined your name day party."

"And you rode all the way up into these dark hills to apologize for that?" he scoffed.

"That and other things," Cara admitted. She hoped her skirt concealed the shaking of her legs.

"Yeah? Like what?" He obviously wasn't going to make it easy for her, and she couldn't blame him.

She clasped her hands behind her back to keep from reaching out for him. He'd rebuff her anyway. "Like not telling you that I was married before, and to whom."

"I find all of this incredible to believe, so let me understand this. You, Cara Sokol, are actually a widow. Okay, you told me about this before, and I was sorry for your loss. And now you *finally* tell me the rest of it—that you are the widow of Constantine Constantinos, one of the richest men in Greece. You inherited a million dollars from him, but are pretending to be an American university student. Why?"

"I'm just as much a college student as you are, Yannis. When were you going to tell me you weren't just a construction foreman? Didn't your aunt say you were top of your class in architecture somewhere in Ohio?"

He shrugged. "That's right. I go to Ohio State University in Columbus. I don't think much about school during the summer, and once we got involved I obviously didn't think about it at all."

Cara winced at his sarcasm. But if he was young enough to still be in college… "How old are you anyway?" she demanded. God, what if he was nineteen? Had she fallen in love with a teenager?

"Twenty-four. I'm finishing my master's degree."

Her sigh of relief was audible in the darkness.

"Why? How old are you?"

"Twenty-eight."

"Ah, an older woman. But not as old as your late husband."

Since he'd brought Con up, she took the opening. "No, I was twenty-two when I met Con, and he was thirty-six. He wanted a wife to produce an heir to his shipping empire, and I wanted a loving husband. Neither of us got what we wanted."

Now that she had found Yannis, the adrenaline surge receded and she sat under the olive tree before her legs gave out.

"Why are you sitting? I didn't ask you to come here, and I don't want you to stay here on my land."

She put her hand on the ancient tree trunk for support and inspiration, silently begging for the words to make him understand, if not forgive. "I want to tell you what happened, and why I was dishonest."

"You know, my family was almost destroyed by lies.

My father had to leave Greece to find work once his cheating business partner wrecked their reputations. I swore I'd never let the same thing happen to me. I didn't have to tell you Gus wanted me to pass along information about the land deal, but I did, because I didn't want any dishonesty between us. And now I find the woman I— Never mind. I don't want to listen to any more lies."

Cara put her hands on her hips. Had he almost said the woman he loved? She stomped over to her borrowed scooter, pushed the ignition button and sent it roaring into a thorn bush, where the motor choked and died. Now she was stuck there until he either listened to her or left her. "I can't keep you here, Yannis. You can race back to town, back to your party, and tell everyone what a deceiving bitch I am. I'll go pack and leave on the ferry tomorrow."

"Crazy! You're crazy!" He walked toward his scooter, and for a long, long minute, she thought he was going to do exactly that. But he made an angry gesture at the machine and stormed back to her. "And what kind of man would I be, eh? To leave a woman alone in the dark out in the country with a broken scooter she probably stole and has no idea how to drive?"

Cara had managed okay, but he was right about the theft.

He went on, "So you tell me what you have to say, and then we both go back to town."

"Thank you, Yannis."

"I don't need your thanks, *Karoleena.*" He leaned nastily on the Greek version of her name. "Unless you want to thank me for all the pleasure I gave you?"

"You got plenty of pleasure of your own, buddy, so don't look for a thank-you card from me!" He'd finally goaded her into losing her cool.

He gave a short chuckle. She took a deep breath and started telling him how she had been a crew member on a charter on Corfu and Con had been a guest of the ship's owner. Tanned, athletic Cara had caught handsome Con's eye and he had bowled her over with his rich worldliness and protestations of love. He'd even insisted on calling her "Karoleena" to give her a sophisticated air.

After a whirlwind courtship, Con married her on his own private island and settled her there with Athena to look after her. Cara took a deep breath before the next part of her story. Yannis's face was set into deep lines, and she was unsure what he made of her.

"So Con headed back to Athens after our honeymoon. I stayed with Athena, who tried to ease me into Greek life. She taught me Greek, not knowing I'd read the tabloids that said that Con was seen at various parties with his longtime companion, Clio Papadopoulos. 'Companion'—at least that's what the Greek dictionary I checked said. 'Mistress' would have been more accurate."

Yannis had been standing unnaturally still and burst into motion, pacing back and forth over the packed ground. "Why didn't you tell me who you were when we were talking last week about Constantine—your husband," he said with a grimace. "Oh, I understand—right before you got your migraine. Was that a pretense, too?"

"No. It was a shock to hear what you thought of me."

"You?" He threw up his hands. "I was talking about some woman my aunt read about in those tabloids. How was I to expect the most infamous widow in Greece was the woman I was sleeping with?"

"And that is exactly why I didn't want to come back. If it hadn't been for Athena being so sick I never would have set foot in Greece again." Cara faced him. "Con picked me as a baby-maker. I was young and healthy, and his mistress was infertile, so she didn't ever expect him to marry her. I didn't get pregnant right away, so he went back to Athens for business and pleasure. Once I found out about his infidelity with Clio, there was little pleasure from me. He promised me several times that he'd ended his affair, but he couldn't keep away from her."

"He preferred someone over you?" Yannis sounded outraged, which was encouraging.

"I still thought I loved him, so I did my best to draw him back to me," she admitted. "I returned to Athens, I straightened my hair and dyed it blond, lost a terrible amount of weight and made myself sick in the process. I stayed out late partying and generally made a fool of myself." She shuddered at her past desperate behavior. "The paparazzi stalked me and one even rammed into the side of my car. In fact," she continued, "when Con died, his family wanted to disinherit me but couldn't. And they treated my husband's mistress as the grieving widow, not me. She couldn't inherit his fortune, after all."

"But you risked coming back to all that? Why?"

"I came for Athena. But I stayed…for you."

"Me?" He straightened up from leaning against the olive tree.

"Yes." Risking the paparazzi was small potatoes compared to what she was risking now. She stood, drawing strength up from her legs like a tree's roots. "I stayed for you because I fell in love with you."

"You don't love me. You wanted a hot Greek guy for the summer, and you got him. Now you can write a nice paper for your English class called, 'Who I Did on My Summer Vacation.'"

Cara winced. His cynicism was out of the ordinary for

him, but not unexpected. "I am sorry for deceiving you. I was a coward for too many years, but meeting you, being with you, *loving* you, forced me to change. To be brave." She stepped forward, pressing her body against his. He tried to move away from her, but the olive tree was at his back and to her advantage. "Oh, Yannis." She twined her arms around his neck. "Yannis *mou, latria mou, fos ton mation mou.*" She told him all the endearments he'd used with her. *"Eime erotevmeni mazi sou."* I'm in love with you. She pressed kisses over his face, continuing to tell him of her love for him. *"S'agapo, Yannis."* Somehow, it was easier to spill her heart to him in his native language.

"You really do speak Greek well." He kept his hands at his sides, but his breathing had sped up.

Encouraged, she kissed his mouth. "These lips will not lie to you again, Yannis. I promise."

He grabbed her shoulders and held her away from him. He stared deeply into her eyes, seemingly intent on arguing more, but then blurted, "Oh, hell," and dragged her close. He lowered his face to hers. *"Cara mou, eime erotevmenos mazi sou.* I love you, too, Cara, despite your million dollars."

"More like twenty million," she muttered just as he was about to kiss her.

"Twenty?" He pulled back, clearly surprised. "Are you joking?"

"I'm trying to give it away, I swear. You know those anonymous Aphrodisias islander scholarships your cousins won?"

"You?" He started to laugh. "Now my uncle really will have a fit."

"I'll send Stav's kids to university, too, if they want."

He cupped her cheek. "Hmm. I guess we do owe that

guy a favor for stranding us at Aphrodite's Grotto. It's a magical place."

Cara shook her head. "The magic was with us all along."

"Yes." His eyes glittered in the moonlight, wild and deep with passion. "You and I."

This time, he actually did kiss her, and she clung to him under the ancient olive tree, the tree that had sheltered two millennia of lovers. It knew its job by now, its leaves whispering songs of love to the man and woman who stood entwined in the shadows of its branches.

Epilogue

"I'M NOT SURE how you're going to carry me over the threshold with this setup." Cara stood with her hands on her hips and stared at the cozy pop-up tent set in Aphrodite's Grotto. Stavros had once again dropped them off at the Grotto, this time willingly and without threat of blackmail. Athena had cut back her meddling with the locals now that she had a whole crop of new people from the university excavation team. More often than not she was found bossing around the student workers, dust covering her black dress as she strode through the dig site. Once the dig was finished, the women's museum would be built nearby to house all the unearthed Aphrodisian temple artifacts, including a beautiful small bronze statue of the goddess carrying of all things, a rose.

"Oh, yes, your quaint American wedding custom." Yannis came up behind her and nuzzled the back of her neck.

"Right, like Athena and your aunt rolling half a dozen local babies over our sleeping bags to ensure our fertility *wasn't* a quaint Greek wedding custom?" Once Aunt Eleni saw how well Gus's new Belgian villa development was selling, she'd forgiven Athena and Cara for ruining the deal Gus had tried to ruin in the first place. After all, what was a little wheeling and dealing among family now?

His white, flashing grin still made her weak in the knees. "Don't worry, I brought plenty of antifertility charms, if you know what I mean." He slipped his hand down to cup her ass. "Want to try one out?"

She spun in his embrace and wrapped her arms around his neck. "You know I do." She gave her husband of one day a sweet, long kiss, hardly believing that two years had passed since their first hot, sexy summer on Aphrodisias. So much had happened. Emma had lived with Niko and his family for a few disastrous weeks that summer before returning to grad school. It had been so bad that sweet, good-natured Emma had learned the Greek curse for the Evil Eye from Athena and used it on Niko's mother as she packed her bags and left. Niko finally got his own place, where he picked up blond tourist girls to his heart's—or some other body part's—content.

Emma had been in fine spirits at Cara's wedding, bringing along her current boyfriend, a mountainous Scot with a Ph.D. in theoretical physics. When he wasn't playing rugby or looking longingly at Emma, the two lovebirds had in-depth conversations where Cara only understood the words, *if, and* and *but*.

Cara and Yannis had both graduated from school and were looking forward to new jobs, dividing their time between Aphrodisias and Athens, Yannis as an architect and Cara as a translator and English teacher. Athens finally felt safe to Cara now that so much time had passed, even more so with Yannis at her side in their cozy apartment.

But the magic island of Aphrodisias would always be their true home. Cara slipped out of his arms and picked up a bouquet of red, white and every color of pink roses specially chosen for a special place. She carried the fragrant bundle to the small alcove behind the spring where a statue of the goddess of Love had once stood—maybe even the small bronze she'd soon see in the museum. Cara laid the flowers on the marble niche, and the summer breeze stilled, the birds quieting in the trees.

"Thank you," she whispered, blowing a kiss. The wind picked up the scent of roses and swirled it around the grotto as Cara returned to her husband, Yannis, hand-delivered seemingly by Aphrodite herself. With more than a little help from Athena.

* * * * *

In honor of our 60th anniversary,
Harlequin® American Romance® is celebrating
by featuring an all-American male each month,
all year long with
MEN MADE IN AMERICA!
This June, we'll be featuring American men living
in the West.

Here's a sneak preview of
THE CHIEF RANGER by Rebecca Winters.

Chief Ranger Vance Rossiter has to confront the sister of
a man who died while under Vance's watch…
and also confront his attraction to her.

"Chief Ranger Rossiter?" The sight of the woman who'd stepped inside Vance's office brought him to his feet. "I'm Rachel Darrow. Your secretary said I should come right in."

"Please," he said, walking around his desk to shake her hand. At a glance he estimated she was in her midtwenties. Her feminine curves did wonders for the pale blue T-shirt and jeans she was wearing. "Ranger Jarvis informed me there's a young boy with you."

The unfriendly expression in her beautiful green eyes caught him off guard. "Yes," was her clipped reply. "When we arrived in Yosemite the ranger told me I couldn't go anywhere in the park until I talked to you first."

"That's right."

"Knowing you wanted this meeting to be private, he offered to show my nephew around Headquarters."

So this woman was the victim's sister…. "What's his name?"

"Nicky."

The boy who haunted Vance's dreams now had a name. "How old is he?"

"He turned six three weeks ago. Were you the man in charge when my brother and sister-in-law were killed?"

"Yes. To tell you I'm sorry for what happened couldn't begin to convey my feelings."

The woman's gaze didn't flicker. "I won't even try to describe mine. Just tell me one thing. Was their accident preventable?"

"Yes," he answered without hesitation.

"In other words, the people working under you fell asleep on your watch and two lives were snuffed out as a result."

Hearing it put like that, he had to set the record straight. "My staff had nothing to do with it. I, myself, could have prevented the loss of life."

Ms. Darrow's expression hardened. "So you admit culpability."

"Yes. I take full blame."

A look of pain crossed over her features. "You can just stand there and admit it?" Her cry echoed that of his own tortured soul.

"Yes." He sucked in his breath.

"I work for a cruise line. Aboard ship, it's the captain's responsibility to maintain rigid safety regulations. If a disaster like that had happened while he was in charge he would have been relieved of his command and never given another ship again."

Rachel Darrow couldn't know she was preaching to the converted. "If you've come to the park with the intention of bringing a lawsuit against me for negligence, maybe you should." It would only be what he deserved.

"Maybe I will."

In the next instant, she wheeled around and hurried out of his office. Vance could have gone after her, but it would cause a scene, something he was loath to do for a variety of reasons. In the first place, he needed to cool down before he approached her again.

The discovery of the Darrows' frozen bodies had affected every ranger in the park. A little boy had been orphaned—a boy whose aunt was all he had left.

* * * * *

Will Rachel allow Vance to explain—
and will she let him into her heart?
Find out in
THE CHIEF RANGER
Available June 2009 from
Harlequin® American Romance®.

We'll be spotlighting a different series every month
throughout 2009 to celebrate our 60th anniversary.

Look for Harlequin®
American Romance® in June!

Join us for a year-long celebration of the rugged
American male! From cops to cowboys—
Men Made in America has the hero
you've been dreaming about!

Look for

The Chief Ranger

by Rebecca Winters, on sale in June!

nocturne™

New York Times Bestselling Author

REBECCA BRANDEWYNE

FROM THE MISTS OF WOLF CREEK

Hallie Muldoon suspects that her grandmother
has special abilities, but her sudden death
forces Hallie to return to Wolf Creek, where
details emerge of a spell cast. Local farmer
Trace Coltrane and the wolf that prowls around
the farmhouse both appear out of nowhere, and
a killer has Hallie in his sights. With no other
choice, Hallie relies on Trace for help,
not knowing if the mysterious Trace is a
mesmerizing friend or a deadly foe....

Available June wherever books are sold.

REQUEST YOUR FREE BOOKS!

2 FREE NOVELS PLUS 2 FREE GIFTS!

HARLEQUIN®

Blaze™

Red-hot reads!

YES! Please send me 2 FREE Harlequin® Blaze™ novels and my 2 FREE gifts (gifts are worth about $10). After receiving them, if I don't wish to receive any more books, I can return the shipping statement marked "cancel". If I don't cancel, I will receive 6 brand-new novels every month and be billed just $4.24 per book in the U.S. or $4.71 per book in Canada. Shipping and handling is just 25¢ per book. That's a savings of 15% or more off the cover price! I understand that accepting the 2 free books and gifts places me under no obligation to buy anything. I can always return a shipment and cancel at any time. Even if I never buy another book, the two free books and gifts are mine to keep forever.

151 HDN ERVA 351 HDN ERUX

Name	(PLEASE PRINT)	
Address		Apt. #
City	State/Prov.	Zip/Postal Code

Signature (if under 18, a parent or guardian must sign)

Mail to the **Harlequin Reader Service:**
IN U.S.A.: P.O. Box 1867, Buffalo, NY 14240-1867
IN CANADA: P.O. Box 609, Fort Erie, Ontario L2A 5X3

Not valid to current subscribers of Harlequin Blaze books.

Want to try two free books from another line?
Call 1-800-873-8635 or visit www.morefreebooks.com.

* Terms and prices subject to change without notice. Prices do not include applicable taxes. N.Y. residents add applicable sales tax. Canadian residents will be charged applicable provincial taxes and GST. Offer not valid in Quebec. This offer is limited to one order per household. All orders subject to approval. Credit or debit balances in a customer's account(s) may be offset by any other outstanding balance owed by or to the customer. Please allow 4 to 6 weeks for delivery. Offer available while quantities last.

Your Privacy: Harlequin Books is committed to protecting your privacy. Our Privacy Policy is available online at www.eHarlequin.com or upon request from the Reader Service. From time to time we make our lists of customers available to reputable third parties who may have a product or service of interest to you. If you would prefer we not share your name and address, please check here. ☐

HB09R

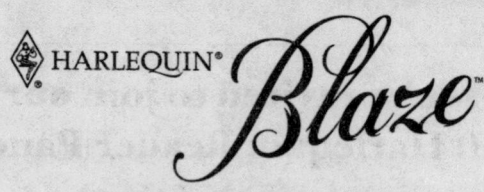

COMING NEXT MONTH
Available May 26, 2009

#471 BRANDED Tori Carrington
Jo Atchison isn't your average cowgirl. She's rough, she's tough and she's sexy as hell. And regardless of the rules, she wants rancher Trace Armstrong. Luckily, Trace wants Jo, too. The only one not happy about it is Jo's volatile boyfriend....

#472 WHEN THE SUN GOES DOWN... Crystal Green
A trip to Japan on family business is just the chance Juliana Thompsen and Tristan Cole have been waiting for. They've been hopelessly in love with each other for years, but a family feud made a relationship impossible. Now they're alone, and they're going to experience *everything* they've missed. But will it be enough to last them a lifetime?

#473 UNDRESSED Heather MacAllister
Encounters
Take some naughty talk, add one *very* thin wall between the last dressing room in a bridal shop and a tuxedo boutique, and what do you have? The recipe for a happy marriage...and four very satisfied—and enlightened—couples. When you get this kind of tailoring, who needs a honeymoon?

#474 TWIN TEMPTATION Cara Summers
The Wrong Bed: Again and Again
Maddie Farrell has just learned she has a twin sister. And she's an heiress. *And* she's just had sex with the hot stranger in her bed! It must be a mistake. Right? Hmm—she might have to have more sex just to make sure....

#475 LETTERS FROM HOME Rhonda Nelson
Uniformly Hot!
Ranger Levi McPherson is getting some anonymous, red-hot love letters during his tour of duty! When he comes home on leave, he's determined to track down the mysterious author...and show her that actions speak louder than words.

#476 THE MIGHTY QUINNS: BRODY Kate Hoffmann
Quinns Down Under
Runaway bride Payton Harwell thinks she's hit rock bottom when she ends up in jail—in Australia! But then sexy rebel Brody Quinn bails her out and lets her into his home, his bed, his life. Only, Payton's past isn't as far away as she thinks it is....